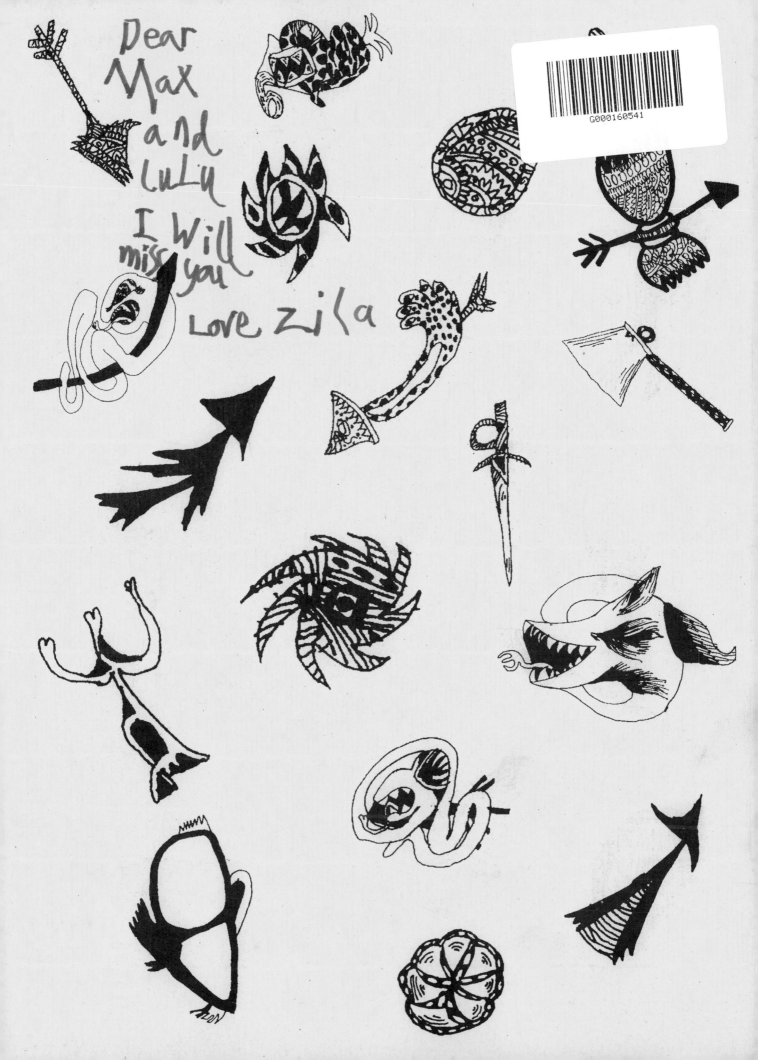

Dear
Max
and
LuLu
I will
miss you
Love zila

Samhita Arni

The Mahabharatha

A Child's View

Part 2

Tara Publishing

Contents

The Second Part

Samhita Arni's Mahabharatha comes in two parts. Part One, as those who have read it will know, begins with the story of King Santanu and ends with the exile of the Pandavas.

Part Two takes over from there. It is really a Book of War, for it shows how everything that happens after the Pandavas are exiled lead them and their cousins, the Kauravas, inevitably to war.

Samhita's descriptions of the battles fought at Kurukshetra are precise, and yet detailed. She displays a wonderful sense of timing in moving from one scene to the next. Her narration of Abhimanyu's death is touching. Her account of Karna's death and Duryodhana's grief is equally moving. The futility of war and the sorrow it causes underwrite her exhaustive descriptions of conflict.

As they get into Part Two of the Mahabharatha, readers will find that it reads and looks different. Samhita's writing and drawing styles have obviously changed. Her tone is terse and urgent. Her illustrations are more dramatic. Every other page breathes war.

Rathna Ramanathan has designed the book to complement Samhita's new perspective. Astras fly off the page, bodies are strewn across paragraphs and characters confront each other in anger and hatred.

We hope readers enjoy Part Two of the Mahabharatha as much as they enjoyed Part One. It does make disturbing reading, gripping in its plot and tragic in tone.

Words marked with an asterisk (*) in the text are explained at the end.

V. Geetha
Gita Wolf   Madras, August 1996

4

The Book of War

When I completed Part One of the Mahabharatha, I thought I deserved a vacation. I began work on Part Two two months later, refreshed from the break. When I wrote Part One, I did so in fits and starts. I did not do the chapters in the correct order. However with Part Two, I was more experienced and organised. I finished writing and illustrating in a little more than four months.

The total number of chapters in Part Two is fifty-five. It covers the thirteen years the Pandavas spent in exile, the Kurukshetra War, and concludes with the last journey of the Pandavas.

Part Two has more characters and events than Part One and I found it difficult to put them together. Sometimes, I am brief in my descriptions, as when I narrate the first nine days of the War. But I have given a detailed account of the last nine days at Kurukshetra. This is because all the brutal fighting and the major battles of the War take place in the last nine days. I have not lingered on subjects such as the Bhagavad Gita or on the advice Bhishma gives Yudhishtira. I have only touched on the moral of the Bhagavad Gita: do your duty. As for Bhishma's advice to Yudhishtira on statecraft and ideal kingship, I feel it may be useful to politicians but not to children. If, however, the reader wants to learn about the duties of a king, he or she can read the book titled "Leadership Secrets" by Meera Oberoi.

I feel my drawing style has improved and the characters in Part Two look more expressive than the ones in Part One. I have put in things such as talcum powder, perfume and a book shelf in the pictures. I feel if a child sees things she knows from daily life, she will enjoy and understand the pictures more.

The Mahabharatha's moral is this: nobody is perfect and all that one strives for may actually be worthless in the end. Yet we are told we must do our duty.

I feel the real message of the Mahabharatha has to do with war. It tells us that war is futile. Though this message has been carried from generation to generation, from century to century, it has gone unheeded. In our century we have waged too many wars and we continue to wage them. These wars have resulted in sadness, poverty, drought and famine. Are we not destroying ourselves?

I feel every deed done in the present will be magnified a thousand times over in the future. The stories in the Mahabharatha make this clear.

I enjoyed writing and illustrating this book. If the reader has any questions, she can write to me or to Tara Publishing. I always want to write to authors but no one gives their addresses in their books.

Samhita Arni   Madras, August 1996

Chapter 1
The Departure
of the Pandavas

The news of the banishment of the Pandavas spread quickly. Accompanied by his son Dhristadyumna, King Draupada came to Hastinapura to bid farewell to the Pandavas and Draupadi.

Krishna also rushed from Dwaraka as soon as he could. Hearing Draupadi's woeful tale, Dhristadyumna's eyes blazed with anger. He promised Draupadi, "I will avenge this insult done to you, Draupadi, even if I die doing so." Krishna promised the Pandavas that he would see every one of those Kauravas wiped out from the face of the earth.

Krishna

Draupadi

7

Draupada and Dhristadyumna soon left, taking with them Draupadi's young sons. Krishna then returned to Dwaraka after a tender parting with the Pandavas. He was accompanied by his sister Subadra, who had married Arjuna, and her son Abhimanyu.

After taking leave of their mother Kunthi, Bhishma and Vidura, the Pandavas journeyed to the Kamyaka forest. They had been told that it was a calm, peaceful place, with only a few detached sages living there.

It was a sad sight to see them leave. All of them had exchanged their magnificent brocade robes for coarse cloth made from the bark of trees.

Yudhishtira led first, covering his eyes with a piece of cloth, for his gaze had the power to burn Hastinapura to ashes. Bhima followed, clenching his powerful fists, wondering why he had not used them when Draupadi was humiliated. Arjuna walked third in line, carelessly kicking up dust, as he would scatter arrows during the inevitable war to come. The twins walked side by side, staring blankly ahead of them. Their faces revealed not the slightest sign of the emotions inside them.

Draupadi made up the rear, her head bent, tears flowing from her eyes and her dark hair, dirty with sand, streaming behind her. The citizens of Hastinapura followed the Pandavas up to the river Ganga and then reluctantly returned to their homes. Some brahmins went with the Pandavas into exile.

Yudhishtira

Bhima

Arjuna

Nakula and
Sahadeva

Draupadi

Chapter 2
The Forest
of Kamyaka

Yudhishtira's penance to Surya

The Pandavas decided to reach the forest of Kamyaka quickly. In no time they had crossed the Ganga. They spent the night at Pramanavata. Soon the problem of food arose. The Pandavas could live on whatever they found in the forest, but the brahmins who followed them were very fussy about what they ate. The Pandavas and Draupadi were in a great dilemma.

Dhaumya, the priest of the Pandavas, advised Yudhishtira to pray to the Sun

God, Surya. Yudhishtira heeded the words of his priest and offered prayers to Surya. Pleased by Yudhishtira's devotion, the generous Surya granted Yudhishtira a boon. He said that he would provide them food for the next twelve years. He gave Yudhishtira a copper vessel and said, "Whenever Draupadi serves out of this vessel, the quantity of the food will be infinite. However, after Draupadi eats, no food will be produced by this vessel until the next meal."

With the acquiring of the magical copper vessel, Yudhishtira was able to solve the problem of food.

Draupadi feeding the Pandavas and their guests

The next day the Pandavas crossed the rivers, Dhrishadvati and Yamuna, and came to the banks of the river Saraswathi. They had reached the forest of Kamyaka.

Chapter 3
Maitreya's Curse

Maitreya

After seeing the plight of the Pandavas in the Kamyaka forest, an enraged sage called Maitreya paid a visit to Dhritarashtra in Hastinapura. In the court of Hastinapura, Maitreya reproached Drona and Bhishma for allowing Shakuni to cheat Yudhishtira in the game of dice. He spoke about the injustice done to the sons of Pandu, who were the rightful heirs to the throne.

Finally, he demanded to see Duryodhana. Dhritarashtra hesitated, and then sent for Duryodhana.

Maitreya requested Duryodhana to recall the Pandavas to Hastinapura and to crown Yudhishtira as king. Maitreya then described the latest deed of Bhima—the killing of Kirmira, who was a much feared demon. A friend of the late Hidimba, Kirmira wanted to seek revenge on Bhima.

But after a tough fight, Bhima killed Kirmira.

However, Duryodhana did not seem to be interested in the good advice Maitreya gave. Displeased by Duryodhana's response, Maitreya cursed the cruel prince. "Bhima's vow will come true. He will break your thighs and kill you. Yet, you will live to see your empire slip from your grasp."

Bhishma, Drona and Dhritarashtra tried to make Maitreya withdraw his curse. But he refused to do so, saying, "If Duryodhana abides by my advice, I am willing to withdraw my curse."

But of course Duryodhana did not heed Maitreya's words.

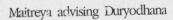

Maitreya advising Duryodhana

Chapter 4
Duryodhana's Shame

Duryodhana travelling to Kamyaka

Duryodhana wondered how the Pandavas were living in Kamyaka. He made an excuse to go there, so that he could taunt and shame the Pandavas. On a fixed date, Duryodhana with his entire retinue of slaves, wives, brothers, friends, and hangers-on reached Kamyaka.

On reaching there, they found themselves obstructed from entering the forest by Chitrasena, a gandharva,* who was a friend of the Pandavas.

Duryodhana was taken captive. A slave escaped Chitrasena's soldiers and reached the Pandavas to tell them about Duryodhana's imprisonment. Yudhishtira, righteous as always, commanded Chitrasena to release Duryodhana. Taken aback, Chitrasena asked why. Yudhishtira answered: "Even though the Kauravas have wronged us, we bear no ill-will against our cousins."

Chitrasena

Pleased with Yudhishtira's answer, Chitrasena released the much shamed Duryodhana. Feeling miserable, Duryodhana returned to Hastinapura. The good deed of the Pandavas only provoked Duryodhana's jealousy. Instead of being grateful, Duryodhana swore that he would avenge this insult.

15

Chapter 5
Arjuna's Decision

The abode of the Pandavas

Finding that the Kamyaka forest was easily accessible to the citizens of Hastinapura, the Pandavas decided to journey to a forest called Dwaitavana.

After a few days, the weary Pandavas arrived at Dwaitavana. They found it peaceful, beautiful and inhabited by a féw sages. Yudhishtira spent most of his time meditating. He found the forest to be the habitat of his dreams, whereas the others found the forest boring. Even though the holy sages treated them well, they were unhappy. They wanted to have their revenge against Duryodhana, and felt they could not be at peace, until their anger had been unleashed.

Thinking of the inevitable war ahead, Arjuna decided to journey to Indrakila, a huge mountain which was an ideal spot for performing penance. Arjuna wanted the divine and powerful Pasupata, the astra* of Shiva. He thought Indrakila would be an ideal place to meditate.

After informing the others of his decision, and on receiving their approval, he bid them goodbye and travelled to Indrakila.

Yudhishtira with the holy sages

17

Chapter 6
Shiva and Arjuna

Arjuna's penance

After a few days travel, Arjuna reached the peak of the great mountain. He found it more serene and beautiful than Dwaitavana. Arjuna built a linga* of Shiva out of clay and prayed to it. He fasted, eating nothing but the berries and leaves which fell from the trees and drinking the cool water of the river flowing nearby.

18

After a few months of fasting and praying, Arjuna found his penance interrupted by a wild boar charging at him. Angered by this disturbance, he sent an arrow at the boar. But as soon as he let go of his bow string, he found that another arrow, not his own, had entered the boar's body at the same time as his.

Turning around, he found a smiling hunter and his wife beseeching him to remove his shaft. The hunter explained he had been in pursuit of the boar for a long time.

Impertinently, Arjuna refused to do so, and was challenged to a duel by the hunter. He agreed, thinking it would only be a matter of time before the hunter was at his mercy. But he was proved wrong. In a few minutes, Arjuna was at the hunter's mercy. But still he fought on, not willing to give in. He prayed to Shiva, who did not seem to be of help.

In an act of desperation, Arjuna threw a hastily made garland of flowers around the linga and turned to face the hunter with renewed strength. But lo! The garland that he had thrown over the linga, appeared around the hunter's neck.

Realising that the hunter was no other than Shiva, Arjuna begged his forgiveness. Shiva smiled and said, "Arjuna, your penance has pleased me. I was testing you to see if you were really worthy of the Pasupata. You have proved yourself able enough to be the owner of it. Therefore I bestow upon you my sacred astra, the fearful Pasupata."

With Shiva's disappearance, the gods of Indralokha appeared and gifted Arjuna their various astras. After receiving the heavenly astras, Arjuna went to Indralokha, his father Indra's abode.

He spent five years there. During that time, he was cursed by Urvashi, the heavenly nymph, to be a eunuch for one year.

Urvashi dancing

Instead of being unhappy, Arjuna found his much needed disguise for the thirteenth year. He learnt dance from his gandharva friend Chitrasena to complete his act. He finally returned to Indrakila where the Pandavas were waiting for him.

Chapter 7
The Deadly Pond

Sahadeva at the pond

The day was extremely hot. The thirsty Pandavas asked Sahadeva to find a pond and inform them. After walking for a while, Sahadeva came upon a pond. As he was about to take a long drink, a voice from nowhere reproached him, saying, "Answer my questions and then drink, for the pond is mine and it will do as I bid it." Sahadeva paused to see where the voice was coming from, and seeing no one, drank the cool, refreshing water. Immediately on drinking the water, Sahadeva collapsed on the banks of the pond, unconscious.

Yama restoring life to the Pandavas

The Pandavas awaited the return of Sahadeva and when he did not come back, they sent Nakula in search of him. As Sahadeva had done before him, Nakula, who also came to the pond, did not heed the words of the invisible being and fell unconscious.

Yudhishtira sent Arjuna, and then Bhima. But the same fate befell them. Finally, Yudhishtira set out in search of his brothers. Like them, he too came upon the pond. On finding his brothers unconscious, he wept and then was about to drink the waters of the lake, when suddenly the voice spoke again.

"Answer my questions before drinking, for the pond is mine and it will do as I bid. Otherwise the fate of your brothers lies ahead of you." Unlike his brothers, Yudhishtira asked, "What are your questions, O Invisible One?"

The mysterious voice asked Yudhishtira a hundred questions, all of which Yudhishtira answered correctly. Pleased by Yudhishtira's answers, the voice asked him, "Which of your brothers do you wish to see restored to life?"

After thinking for a long time, Yudhishtira answered, "My brother, Nakula." The voice then proceeded to ask "Why?" Yudhishtira replied, "For at least I, one of Kunthi's children, am alive and it would be fitting for Madri's line to be carried on as well."

The invisible being then restored to Yudhishtira not only Nakula but all the four brothers. Then the area around the pond was lit by a blinding light and a godlike being stepped out of a shining chariot. The divine being said, "I am Yama*, your father, Yudhishtira! I have tested you, my son, and have seen that you are the very essence of righteousness. Yes, I was the voice. I have come to advise you to go to Matsya, where the good and wise King Virata lives. You will not be discovered until the period of the exile is over."

Yama vanished, leaving the Pandavas astounded.

Chapter 8
Preparation for the Years of Disguise

Bhima as Valala

The Pandavas decided on their various disguises before they set out for Matsya. Yudhishtira decided to disguise himself as a Brahmin who had seen prosperity at one time. He called himself Kanka. Bhima, who made excellent meals, decided to go as a cook. He named himself Valala.

Arjuna put to use Urvashi's curse and became a eunuch skilled in dancing. He covered his scars, made by the continual use of weapons, with conch bracelets. His name was to be Brihannala.

Nakula said he would be a groom in Virata's stable and his name would be Damagranthi. Sahadeva said he would be a cowherd and offer to look after Virata's cows. He would call himself Tantripala. Draupadi gave herself the name of Sairandhri. She would be Queen Sudeshna's hair dresser, and have five gandharvas as husbands. Having disguised themselves thus, the Pandavas proceeded to Matsya.

When they reached the outskirts of Virata's kingdom, they tied their weapons in cowhide and hung the bundle up on a tree. This way, the weapons would be safe, for people would think the bundle was a corpse and not touch it, for fear of being polluted.

In order not to cause suspicion, they entered Matsya on different days.

Draupadi as Sairandhri

Chapter 9
Kichaka

Kichaka running after
Draupadi

The real ruler of Matsya, the power behind the throne, was Kichaka, Queen Sudeshna's brother and Virata's commander-in-chief.

Kichaka saw Draupadi and was enamoured of her. Finding himself infatuated by Draupadi's beauty, he asked his sister Sudeshna if he could have the so-called Sairandhri as his slave. Sudeshna had heard that her maid had five gandharvas as her husbands. She feared for her brother and reproached Kichaka. But his desire did not vanish and he grew pale and ill. Finally, in an impulsive moment, Sudeshna handed a golden goblet of rich

26

golden wine to Draupadi and commanded her to carry it to Kichaka's apartments. Draupadi pleaded with the Queen to send somebody else, but Sudeshna remained firm.

Rather reluctantly, Draupadi carried the goblet of wine to Kichaka's quarters. Kichaka, having been informed of Sudeshna's plan earlier, had perfumed and dressed himself for the occasion. Some women would have found him hard to resist, but with Draupadi, it was not so. Realising Kichaka's intentions, Draupadi set down the heavily carved goblet on a table hastily and fled the place. The goblet rocked to and fro causing the golden wine to spill.

Kichaka hurriedly picked up his trailing garments and followed Draupadi. Draupadi reached Virata's court, where Virata and Yudhishtira were immersed in a conversation. She fell at Virata's feet, begging for his protection.

Being a very weak mortal, and afraid of Kichaka, Virata said nothing. However, Draupadi managed to avoid the infatuated Kichaka for the moment.

That night, dressed in black, Draupadi secretly visited Bhima. He had not heard of the Kichaka incident, and was immensely angry when Draupadi related her tale of woe.

Bhima devised a quick but effective plan. He told Draupadi to invite Kichaka to the dancing hall at midnight on the day of the full moon. Draupadi passed on the message to Kichaka who was overjoyed.

Draupadi

27

He grew impatient. On the night of the full moon, he perfumed himself with musk, applied sandal wood on his arms and legs and wore pure white garments. He went to the dancing hall at the stroke of midnight. On reaching the hall, he perceived a figure lying on a couch, covered with a white cloth.

Thinking that the figure on the couch was Draupadi, he tiptoed to the couch and whispered, "Sairandhri, is that you?" In response to his question, a powerful hand, with a grip of iron, seized Kichaka's arm. Realising that the sinews on the arm were not Draupadi's, he drew back the white sheet.

"Valala!" Kichaka screamed.

Bhima, in his gruff, husky voice said, "No, its Bhima. You have disgraced my wife, Draupadi, and I wish to kill you." Saying this, he strangled Kichaka, pummelling him into a squashy, disfigured corpse. He then bundled Kichaka into a white sheet.

The next day the palace guards found Kichaka in the dancing hall. They rushed to the court and informed the king of Kichaka's death. Yudhishtira raised his eyebrows on hearing the palace guards' tale, realising that the killing technique was Bhima's. He agreed wholeheartedly with Bhima's decision.

Virata was dismayed on hearing of Kichaka's death. He knew his military strength was diminished. It was a great loss to Matsya. The funeral rites were performed.

Everybody turned suspicious eyes on Sairandhri, who said that her five gandharva husbands had avenged her disgrace. Queen Sudeshna wanted to dismiss Draupadi. But Draupadi pleaded with Sudeshna to let her remain for another two months. She claimed that her gandharva husbands would be under a curse for that period. So Sudeshna let her remain for another two months as her maid.

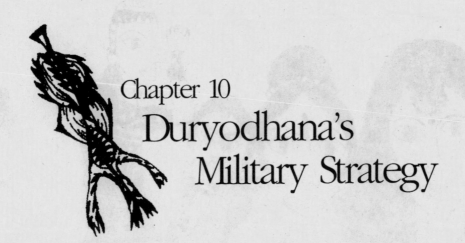

Chapter 10
Duryodhana's Military Strategy

Susharma

Duryodhana got the news of Kichaka's death. Realising that Matsya would be a good addition to his growing empire, he and Karna planned to conquer Matsya. Karna, who was wiser than Duryodhana, realised that the woman claiming to have five gandharvas as husbands was probably Draupadi. The technique used to kill Kichaka was that of Bhima's. So Duryodhana convened a meeting of his evil allies to devise a military strategy.

King Susharma was one of the famous Trigarta brothers who bore a vengeance against Kichaka and Matsya. Again and again Kichaka had plagued his kingdom. Now, along with Duryodhana, Susharma decided to attack Matsya. He was to attack Matsya from the north and steal Virata's cows. By doing so, he hoped to lure out the Pandavas and a large section of the Matsyan army. After a day, the Kaurava army was to invade Matsya from the south, and try to conquer it.

Uttara Kumar showing off his strength

Only Drona and Bhishma disagreed with Karna's plan. But being loyal to their regent, Dhritarashtra, they agreed to participate in the unjust battle.

The Kauravas' war strategy worked, at first. The Trigarta brothers marched on Matsya and stole Virata's cows. Realising he was without a good general, Virata was in absolute despair. Kanka came to his rescue. He said, "When the Pandavas were reigning in Indraprastha, Valala, Damagranthi, Tantripala and myself were in their service. We were generals in Yudhishtira's army and are excellent in the art of weapons."

Virata was grateful to his four servants who agreed to be his generals.

Virata and his hastily appointed generals marched forth to defeat the Trigarta brothers.

Meanwhile, the Kaurava army attacked Matsya from the south. The entire Matsyan army was fighting in the north. There was only the young prince Uttara Kumar left to protect Matsya. He was basically a coward and a wimp. But now, he boasted he would protect Matsya. The ladies-in-waiting at the palace were very impressed with their prince. Since everyone had gone with Virata, the problem of a charioteer came up. Draupadi suggested that Uttara Kumar take the eunuch Brihannala. She said, "He has accompanied Arjuna several times and his fame as a charioteer is known all over Indraprastha."

Uttara Kumar laughed at this, but nevertheless proclaimed Brihannala as his charioteer. In a short while, Arjuna and Uttara Kumar were ready to leave.

After bidding farewell to the court ladies, the duo went on their way. After riding a short distance from the town, Arjuna stopped the chariot near a tree which had a bundle strung on one of its branches. He bid Uttara Kumar remove the bundle. Uttara Kumar was repulsed by Arjuna's command. "Chi! That must be a corpse! You expect me to bring that down? You don't know what evil spirits may be found inside it." To this, Arjuna replied, "It's only cowhide. The Pandavas have kept their various weapons here."

यहाँ एक मरा हुआ आदमी है

Uttara Kumar climbing the tree

Uttara Kumar reluctantly climbed the tree.

He removed the bundle. He gave it to Arjuna, who opened it and looked at the various weapons that were there. Uttara Kumar's eyes widened as he saw Bhima's mace, Arjuna's Gandiva*, Nakula and Sahadeva's swords.

Arjuna removed his favourite bow, the Gandiva, from the assorted weapons. He twanged the bowstring. A powerful sound escaped the Gandiva.

Hearing the sound, the Kaurava army was convulsed with dread. They wanted to turn back. But on Duryodhana's bidding, they remained to fight.

Uttara Kumar and Brihannala rode on to confront Duryodhana.

Chapter 11
The Battle between Duryodhana and Arjuna

Uttara Kumar advanced on, but when he caught sight of Duryodhana's great army, his courage left him and he threw down his bow. Arjuna stopped the chariot and bid Uttara Kumar resume his original position. But the young prince was too frightened to fight. So Arjuna revealed his true identity and requested Uttara Kumar to be his charioteer.

The prince, scared out of his wits, agreed and exchanged places with Arjuna.

Arjuna as Brihannala

Uttara Kumar and Arjuna

He had heard so much about Arjuna, but could not believe that the eunuch who taught his sister dance was actually the great and revered warrior. He fell at Arjuna's feet and begged forgiveness and protection. Arjuna merely said, "Please, Prince, take the horses' reins. If we want to drive Duryodhana out of your father's kingdom, we must face them."

So Uttara Kumar gave the horses a kick. The pair of horses, fast as the wind and fierce as fire, charged through the numerous ranks of Duryodhana's soldiers.

Then Arjuna asked Uttara Kumar to stop. He released three arrows. One fell at Kripa's feet, the other at Drona's, and the third at Bhishma's.

They recognised Arjuna and accepted his greetings. Arjuna shot arrows in all directions, destroying anyone who came in his path. Shakuni and Karna feared for Duryodhana, and sent a whole battalion to protect him.

The ranks of the Kaurava army were thinning fast. Karna's horses and charioteer were shot, and his chariot destroyed. He was therefore forced to abandon the battle.

Arjuna's conch

In the meantime, the restless Duryodhana entered the fray. He was promptly joined by the chariotless Karna. Duryodhana now realised that it was none other than Arjuna who was routing his army. As he was about to mention this to the elders, Arjuna blew his conch.

Bhishma, anticipating Duryodhana's information, smiled and said, "Duryodhana, it is none other than Arjuna, as you thought, but..." The Prince of the Kauravas interrupted Bhishma and joyously said, "So we have caught them now. They have to be in exile for another thirteen years." "But let me continue," said the veteran Bhishma, "the moment Arjuna blew his conch was the moment the Pandavas' exile ended."

"The year is not yet up!" responded Duryodhana.

"Yes, it is. But, look! Arjuna seems to be approaching us. He wants to take revenge on you. So let us return to Hastinapura." Disappointed, Duryodhana obeyed the words of Bhishma and returned to Hastinapura.

Chapter 12
The Return
of the Victorious Duo

Virata and Kanka

A messenger ran into the presence of the anxious King Virata, saying, "The young prince Uttara Kumar has emerged victorious, after fighting single-handedly with the renowned warriors Karna, Drona, Ashwathama, Kripa, Dushasana, Duryodhana and Bhishma. At this moment, he is leading the cows through the outskirts of the city."

The overjoyed Virata said to Yudhishtira, "Kanka, let us play a game of chess until my wonderful son arrives."

36

Bleeding Yudhishtira

"I told you that you had nothing to fear with Brihannala as his charioteer" replied Yudhishtira. "A game of chess is always bad for a happy man. If we play, let there be no stakes."

"So be it." the king said. The chess board was laid out and the king shook the dice saying, "My great son has defeated warriors like Bhishma and Karna. He must really be an expert at fighting."

"With Brihannala as his charioteer, even the most cowardly man would have been victorious," responded Yudhishtira.

"Brihannala, Brihannala, Brihannala, that stupid eunuch! What can she do?" exclaimed the angry Virata, as he threw the dice at Yudhishtira's face. Draupadi quickly brought a cup so that Yudhishtira's blood would not fall on the ground.

"Why do you wipe that gambler's face with your silken robe?" questioned King Virata.

"If one drop of this righteous man's blood falls on the ground, it means

37

one year of famine for your land. I am doing you a favour by wiping Kanka's blood," answered Draupadi. At that moment, a doorkeeper announced that Brihannala and Uttara Kumar had arrived. Yudhishtira whispered to the doorkeeper to keep Brihannala away and to let only Prince Uttara Kumar enter.

The Prince was admitted first. Arjuna had instructed him earlier not to reveal his true identity. So when his father praised him, he said, "It was no feat of mine, Father, for a God's son came and took my place. He and Brihannala defeated the Kaurava army."

King Virata wanted to reward the man, but Uttara Kumar said he had disappeared.

Later, Arjuna entered Virata's court. Virata smiled and thanked him for having been a charioteer to his son. While leaving, Arjuna tried to catch Yudhishtira's eye, but the latter kept his face turned away. He did not want to reveal the wound caused by the dice. Arjuna would undoubtedly kill the king who had inflicted it.

A sad Arjuna returned to the women's apartments to teach Uttara music and dance.

Chapter 13
The Pandavas Reveal Their Identities

Yudhishtira and Draupadi

On a glorious morning, the Pandavas and Draupadi dressed themselves in their best clothes and perfumed their bodies with rare sandalwood.

The king and the courtiers were startled when the Pandavas and Draupadi entered the court, for they had never seen a more handsome group of people.

39

"Who are you?" asked the king.

"I am Yudhishtira. Your cook Valala is Bhima, Brihannala is no other than Arjuna. Damagranthi is Nakula and Tantripala is Sahadeva. Sairandhri is my Queen, Draupadi, famed for her lustrous eyes."

Prince Uttara Kumar flashed a knowing smile at the entire assembly.

Bhima

He said, "Father, the God's son was no other than Arjuna, who defeated the Kaurava armies."

The grateful king replied, "I thank you for saving my son. As a reward, I give you the hand of my daughter, Princess Uttara."

"Since I am her teacher, I cannot be her spouse," said Arjuna, "But being a prince, I cannot refuse your offer. My son Abhimanyu is handsome and an expert at handling weapons. He will be happy to marry your daughter."

Draupadi's sons, the entire Vrishni* clan, the Panchala princes and Draupada journeyed to Matsya to witness Abhimanyu's marriage to Uttara. The Pandavas had with them all their friends and allies.

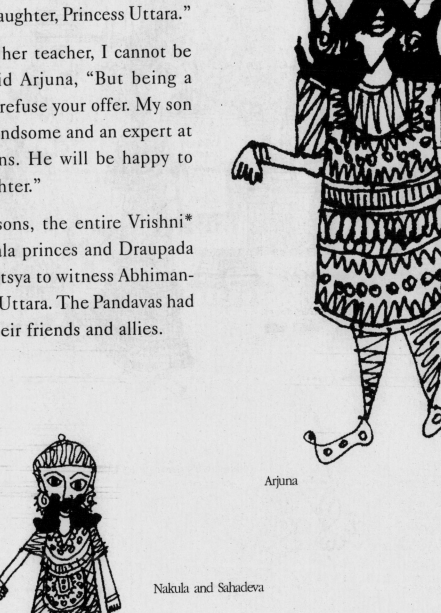

Arjuna

Nakula and Sahadeva

41

Abhimanyu's marriage to Uttara

Chapter 14
The War Council

The tents

The peaceful, nearly uninhabited Matsyan village of Upaplavya was turned into a war camp. For Yudhishtira's allies had assembled there to discuss their future plans. Balarama, the Vrishni king, stood up and proposed a plan. "I say we begin with a peaceful approach. We will ask for the

43

The war council

return of your lands and if Duryodhana doesn't comply, we will then wage war against him."

Krishna seconded Balarama's plan and said, "Balarama is right. Let us send a neutral messenger, such as a member of the Vrishni clan, who is related both to the Pandavas and the Kurus. Let us ask for the return of your entire kingdom. If Dhritarashtra does not agree, let us ask for Indraprastha and four other villages."

Yudhishtira liked the idea. He said, "For those of you who have not been listening, we have decided to send Krishna as envoy to the Kuru* court, where he will ask Dhritarashtra to return my kingdom. If Duryodhana is not willing to let go of it, we will ask for five villages only. If that is not complied with, we will declare war on Duryodhana."

The kings, realising that this was the most ideal and the wisest approach, approved of the plan.

Duryodhana, however, got wind of the meeting at Upaplavya, and assembled the armies of his own allies and vassals.

Chapter 15
Duryodhana's Refusal

Krishna

Krishna duly arrived in Hastinapura and was immediately granted an audience with the king.

King Dhritarashtra received Krishna with high respect, and asked why he had come.

"I have come as an envoy," replied Krishna after a pause, "from the Pandavas. I am on a peaceful mission. All the Pandavas want is their kingdom back. They do not wish to harm their cousins, the Kauravas."

"No!" refused Duryodhana. "We cannot return the Pandavas their kingdom."

"Then, at least give them Indraprastha and four other villages," pleaded Krishna.

46

The Kurus

"No! I will not even give them a needle point of my territory!" cried Duryodhana.

"Well, if that's the way you look at it, the Pandavas declare war on you!" said Krishna rising. "I tell you the forthcoming war is inevitable, after what you did to them. You will be killed in this war, like Bhima vowed and Maitreya cursed!"

Chapter 16
Shalya

Shalya

Shalya, king of Madra and Madri's brother, and therefore uncle to the Pandavas, was on his way to the Pandavas' war camp, with an akshauhini* of his army to help them.

On the way he halted to rest for the night. Every whim of his army was provided for in a trice, by an unknown source. He inhaled the wafting smell of delicious meat served up by his benefactors. Shalya, presuming it was the Pandavas who had met his needs, sent for the provider and declared he would grant him a boon. The tent flap opened—and in walked Duryodhana! Shalya was taken aback and granted Duryodhana a boon.

Shalya at camp

"All I want is you and your akshauhini to be part of my army," said the crafty prince. Shalya's heart sank. Of the million and one things possible, why did Duryodhana ask for this? He begged leave of Duryodhana, for he had to go and see the Pandavas.

At Upaplavya, he told Yudhishtira of Duryodhana's request. "I was foolish to promise him a boon. Now look at what he has done. I am sorry, Yudhishtira," sobbed Shalya.

"Uncle, it is all right, but grant me a boon too." said Yudhishtira. "I will not hesitate to grant you a boon," replied Shalya. "What is it you want, Yudhishtira?"

"All I ask for is this," said Yudhishtira, "When the fateful day of the combat between Karna and Arjuna arrives, you, an experienced charioteer, will be asked to hold Karna's reins. Please strike fear in his heart."

"Of course," sighed Shalya, "I only wish I could do more for you, you poor unfortunate boys."

With a heavy heart, Shalya left Yudhishtira and returned to Hastinapura.

49

Chapter 17
A Charioteer or His Army?

Arjuna

Duryodhana and Arjuna left to ask a boon of their Vrishni cousin, Krishna. Duryodhana arrived first, followed by Arjuna.

Duryodhana sat down on an ornate chair next to the cot on which Krishna was sleeping.

Arjuna placed himself on a lowly stool at the end of Krishna's cot.

Krishna awoke to find Arjuna at his feet. He then turned around and saw Duryodhana.

Duryodhana spoke first. "Since we are both related to you, we have come to ask you to join our armies. I arrived first, so you should join my army."

"But I saw Arjuna first," replied Krishna,

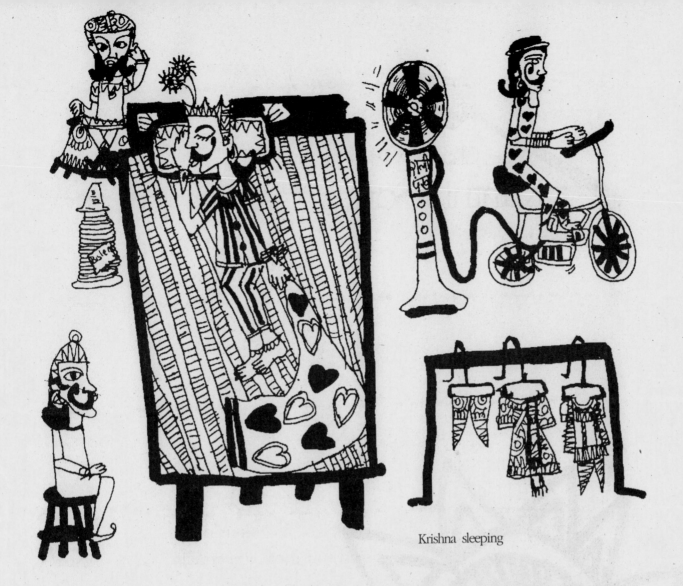

Krishna sleeping

"Anyway, I have an offer. I will be a charioteer to anyone who wants my services or you can have my entire Vrishni army. Think carefully. A charioteer or his army. Arjuna, since I saw you first, which do you choose?"

"I choose you, my lord," said Arjuna. "I will take your army gladly," said an overjoyed Duryodhana, getting up to leave.

On his way to Hastinapura, Duryodhana visited Balarama to request him to be a part of his army. Balarama refused, since he could not fight his brother Krishna. "I will remain neutral, since I love you and Krishna, and I feel torn between you both," he said. Duryodhana however, managed to enlist the support of the great Vrishni hero, Kritavarma and his entire army.

Now Duryodhana had assembled eleven akshauhini and Yudhishtira, seven. The war was to be fought at the battlefield of Kurukshetra.

51

Chapter 18
Kunthi's Son

The sun god

On the eve of the great Kurukshetra battle, Kunthi felt a heartache for her eldest son, Karna.

Used to her orders being carried out with unquestioning obedience by her sons, Kunthi did not even stop to think whether Karna possessed this quality. She reached the spot where Karna usually offered prayers to the setting sun.

She waited, until he had completed his austerities and said, "Karna, I, Kunthi, am your mother and the Sun God is your father..."

"I know that, Kunthi, for Surya appeared to me in a dream and told me who my real parents are," interrupted Karna.

"You know that!" exclaimed Kunthi, surprised. "As I was saying," she continued, "the Pandavas are your younger brothers and, by the rules of matrimony, when an unmarried maiden with a child marries, the child automatically becomes the husband's first child. So, you are Pandu's first-born."

"But you left me, abandoned on a river. I was found by Adiratha and Radha became my mother. I am also called Radheya, Radha's son."

"All that is Yudhishtira's, will be yours. Draupadi will be your wife, Indraprastha your kingdom." said Kunthi.

Kunthi and Karna

"Duryodhana has given me his friendship," answered Karna. "He depends on me to win this war. I cannot leave him. However, I will let all your sons, except Arjuna, live. We will meet in a battle and one of us will die. Either way, you will have five sons."

Kunthi left, feeling infinitely sad, knowing Karna had made his choice. Mother and son embraced each other tenderly, for the first and the last time.

Chapter 19
Sanjaya

Sanjaya was the blind Dhritarashtra's charioteer. Besides Vidura, he was the person Dhritarashtra loved and trusted best. Vyasa visited Dhritarashtra, who complained that he would not be able to see, or even hear about the frightening war that was to take place. Vyasa thought for a while and asked Dhritarashtra whether he would honestly like to see the battles in the war. For he had the power to restore sight to the blind king for the duration of the war.

Vyasa and Dhritarashtra

"No!" replied Dhritarashtra, "for I would not like to see the death of my sons with my own eyes. But I would like it, if somebody could tell me about the events taking place in the war."

Vyasa hesitated before he spoke again. "Sanjaya, I grant you divine sight, the power to see the events on the battlefield of Kurukshetra, even if you are a thousand leagues away from the place.

Sanjaya acquires divine sight

I also give you the power to narrate the accounts of the battle clearly, describing every detail explicitly and impartially."

Sanjaya closed his eyes. Vyasa passed his hands over them.

Chapter 20
Karna's Abdication

Duryodhana and his allies

On the eve of the battle, Duryodhana held a council of war with his elders and allies. On a unanimous vote, Bhishma was chosen as the

Karna

commander-in-chief of the Kaurava forces. Under him, Duryodhana thought the way to victory was ensured. Accepting the honour, Bhishma's eye swept over the entire council and alighted on one solitary figure—Karna.

"I will not fight beside that sutaputra!*" said Bhishma, with great venom in his voice. "His power lies in appeasing you, Duryodhana, with empty words and promises. He will be the end of you, Duryodhana, I am warning you. He is under a curse by Parashurama to fight with Arjuna, and Arjuna is far superior to him. I will not fight beside him."

Karna's eyes blazed. "If that is how you feel, Bhishma, I definitely do not consider it any pleasure fighting beside you. I am sorry Duryodhana, but I will not fight alongside Bhishma. Only after he has fallen, shall I fight in your army. As long as he is alive and commands your army, I will not take up arms beside him."

With his head held high, Karna walked out of the tent. He had abdicated his responsibilities for the moment and would not fight, unless Bhishma laid down his arms or was incapacitated.

For the next ten days, he only watched the events taking place on the battlefield of Kurukshetra.

57

Chapter 21
Arjuna's Sorrow

The sun had risen and covered everything and everybody on the battlefield of Kurukshetra in its warm golden light.

A pleasant breeze blew gently. Colourful pennants and banners flapped in the wind. Arjuna's ape banner was there, with Hanuman's presence adorning it. For Hanuman* had promised his brother Bhima to preside over Arjuna's banner and thus ensure the victory of the Pandavas. Colourful silks were sported by various heroes on the battlefield. There was Arjuna's blue silk, a lovely contrast to that of his charioteer, Krishna, whose silk was a bright yellow. Duryodhana sported a fiery red and Bhishma an unusual electrifying blue.

Hanuman

As the two armies advanced, Arjuna suddenly found himself caught up in a storm of emotions. Sadness, disbelief and sorrow governed him, and in a fit of despair, he threw down his weapons and sat with his head in his hands.

58

Arjuna in distress

Since they were waiting only for the word to attack, Krishna dropped the reins of his horses and turned to Arjuna. Arjuna was distressed.

He said: "I look at the entire Kaurava army and I know everyone there. I see Bhishma with his innumerable battle scars, my teachers Drona and Kripa, my friends Kritavarma and Ashwathama, my uncle Shalya. I see my cousins Duryodhana, Dushasana, Vikarna. I see my nephews. I don't want to kill all these people, even though Duryodhana and the others are willing to kill me. I think of how much sorrow their deaths will bring me. I now can understand why Yudhishtira was willing to settle for five meagre villages. I didn't know that my courage and strength would fail me, when I needed it most. Oh Krishna! I just don't want to fight and kill all these people I've known since my birth." With this, Arjuna burst into tears.

Krishna tried to pacify him. "We are all here on this battlefield to achieve a purpose for which we were created. A long time ago, Mother Earth complained to me, saying that the earth had too many evil men on it. And I was born on earth to help ease the burden of Mother Earth. You were

59

born to help me. We are the divine sages, Nara and Narayana, reborn to rid this world of evil. And through this war we will achieve just that."

"But I don't want to kill anybody," said Arjuna obstinately. "I might seem to hate the Kauravas from outside, but I actually love them. Please help me."

Krishna said, "Arjuna, we are all born with a purpose. You and your brothers are my instruments, to carry out what has already been ordained. You will just kill the mortal bodies of Bhishma and Drona, whereas their souls will live forever and ever. You are releasing them from the cycle of life. They have lived long enough to see your brothers and your cousins grow up. Their duty is over. You might not know it, but they are just waiting for their own end."

"Arjuna," continued Krishna, "It is your duty to relieve this earth of evil minds, such as Duryodhana, Dushasana, Alambusha, Jayadratha and Shakuni. And whatever said and done, that is your duty. Anything or anybody who tries to stop you must also be killed. Duty is

Vishwa:roopa

duty. You have to do your duty, regardless of its consequences. Yes, good people will die, but you will have to sacrifice them for duty."

Arjuna then asked Krishna to show him his Vishwaroopa*. Krishna enveloped himself and Arjuna in a brilliant light and revealed his true form to Arjuna. It was awesome.

The trees made up Krishna's hair. The mountains were his bones. The sun and moon were his eyes. The clouds were his skin. Krishna had four arms. One held the conch, one the chakra, one held the sacred lotus, while the other hand blessed Arjuna. The Gods headed by Indra, the seven great sages and other holy and wise men rose from Krishna's arms.

Krishna proclaimed, "I am the Preserver of all creatures. I am Vishnu."

The shudras bowed to Vishnu at his feet, vaishyas at his knees. The kshatriyas bowed to Vishnu, level with his waist and the brahmins at his chest.

Arjuna was ecstatic at seeing the Vishwaroopa of Vishnu. He said: "Krishna, the light from your body is blinding. Could you return to your normal form?"

Vishnu's lips parted to give Arjuna a smile of infinite charm and purity. In a trice, Krishna was holding the reins of Arjuna's chariot once more

Arjuna asked Krishna, "There are two ways to reach you. What are they?"

Krishna smiled again and said, "The two ways to reach me are through prayer and penance, and through living a normal life, but by doing your duty first. Both kinds of people will reach me when their souls are released. They are both my devotees and I treat them equally!"

Thus appeased, and knowing that his duty came first, Arjuna rushed headlong into battle, blowing his conch and uttering his mighty battle cry.

Chapter 22
Yudhishtira's Request

Yudhistira

As the two armies advanced, Yudhishtira suddenly bid his charioteer stop. Throwing down his weapons, he walked through the ranks of the Kaurava army and came to Bhishma's chariot. He said, "O revered warrior, my grandfather, O celibate one, I seek your blessing to emerge victorious in this war."

Bhishma smiled, and in his gruff voice said, "I am pleased you have asked me for my blessing. Hence all my blessings are with you."

Yudhishtira turned to Drona and made the same request of him. Drona said, "Yudhishtira, had you not come to me for my blessing, I would have cursed you. Since you have come, I bless you."

Yudhishtira then went to his uncle Shalya and friend Kritavarma and asked them to pray for his victory, which they readily consented to do.

Yudhishtira returned to his chariot and picked up his weapons. Just before the two armies attacked each other, Yuyutsu, Dhritarashtra's son by a vaishya woman, stepped out from the ranks of the Kauravas and said in distaste, "I leave the army of my brothers." He joined the Pandavas and continued to fight on their side throughout the war.

The day ended to the advantage of the Kauravas, who won the first day's battle.

Bhishma in his chariot

64

Chapter 23
Bhishma's Promise

Duryodhana reprimands Bhishma

Not happy with his victory on the first day of the war, Duryodhana called on Bhishma, the commander-in chief of his army.

"What is this?" he raged, "Even though we won today, you did not even try to attack the Pandavas. You merely killed a few princes of Matsya.

How can we win this war if you just sit back, leaving the work to soldiers whose self-esteem will vanish, seeing you behave so?"

"Duryodhana," said Bhishma, his eyes closed, "I have told you, time and again, that the Pandavas cannot be defeated. I love you and them equally. I cannot kill them because I love them, and even if I wanted to kill them, I would be killed in the attempt. However, Duryodhana, I promise you that I will kill ten thousand warriors of Yudhishtira's army everyday."

For the next few days, Bhishma stuck to his promise, and killed ten thousand men belonging to the Pandava army.

In the Pandava camp, on the eve of the second day of war, defeated warriors sat in silence, while the Pandavas and their allies mourned the deaths of the brave Matsyan princes, Sveta and Uttara Kumar.

Chapter 24
Battle for Nine days

The Pandavas, who had suffered defeat on the first day of the war, were worried about the second day. Through their heroic efforts, the setting sun saw their victory. The Kauravas saw defeat that day.

A kaurava thinks of Arjuna

On the third day, Arjuna stole the entire show with his prowess. Duryodhana fell unconscious and was taken away by his charioteer. The entire Kaurava army was in disarray. Afterwards, Duryodhana re-grouped his troops. However the day did not prove to be good for the Kauravas. The defeated Kaurava soldiers returned to their camp, impressed with Arjuna's skills. An enraged Duryodhana once more reprimanded Bhishma, who himself had been threatened by Krishna that day. Krishna had rushed out of his chariot, discus in hand, ready to slay Bhishma, since Arjuna would not do so.

Battles raged like forest fires on the fourth day. However, once again, the Pandavas won.

Duryodhana censured Bhishma, yet again. A tired Bhishma advised Duryodhana to end the war.

On the fifth and sixth days the spirits of the soldiers on both sides were low. Neither side won.

On the dawn of the seventh day, Duryodhana approached Bhishma as usual and harassed him. Bhishma again promised to do his best. Yudhishtira asked the same thing of Shikandin, knowing of his vow. "Why is Bhishma not dead? Why have you not killed him? You are born to kill him."

On the eighth day, there were great losses on the Kaurava side. Shakuni's son and many of the Kaurava brothers were killed. The Pandavas suffered the loss of Iravat, Arjuna's son by the Naga Princess, Ulupi. Iravat was killed in a maya* battle, by the asura* Alambusha. Karna, Duryodhana, and Dushasana warned Bhishma that if he did not improve his fighting style, he would no longer be general.

On the ninth day, Krishna attempted to kill Bhishma with his whip, after watching him decimate the Pandava army. Arjuna brought him back to the chariot. On the whole, the honours of the ninth day lay with the Kauravas.

Alambusha and Iravat

Chapter 25
Bhishma
Lies Down

The Pandavas steal out

It was a dark night. Five unarmed figures advanced towards Bhishma's tent, in the Kaurava camp.

When the tent flap opened, they entered. In the lamplight, they removed their cloaks to reveal their identities. They were no other than the five Pandavas.

Bhishma smiled and said, "What can I do for you? Ah, it is good to see you here, rather than on the battlefield."

"Bhishma, our forces are being vanquished by you. We need to know how you can be killed, so that we can win this war."

Bhishma smiled again, "That is an easier task than you think. All you have to do is place Shikandin in front of me and Arjuna behind him. Since she was a woman in her previous birth and spent part of her present life being a woman, I cannot and will not confront Shikandin."

Yudhishtira thanked him. The Pandavas departed from the Kaurava camp.

The next morning, Yudhishtira placed Shikandin in front, with Arjuna behind him. Arjuna was heavily guarded, with Yudhamanyu protecting the left wheel and Uttamaujas the right wheel of his chariot.

They approached Bhishma. Duryodhana had heard of the Pandavas coming to the camp and the nature of their discussion with Bhishma, through his efficient spy system. Although he wanted Bhishma out of the way, he loved the old man and protected him with Kaurava heroes. Dushasana was assigned the task of getting his brothers and allies in formation and arranging them around Bhishma.

Bhishma's tent

71

Duryodhana protected Bhishma for sometime, but was soon wounded. Dushasana's charioteer and horses were killed, his mace broken, and he was thus incapacitated.

Shikandin started firing at Bhishma, who ignored him. From behind him, Arjuna shot arrows which sunk deep into Bhishma's flesh. But the old veteran felt nothing, and as the streams of blood mingled and flowed, the warrior was covered in crimson. He looked like the setting sun.

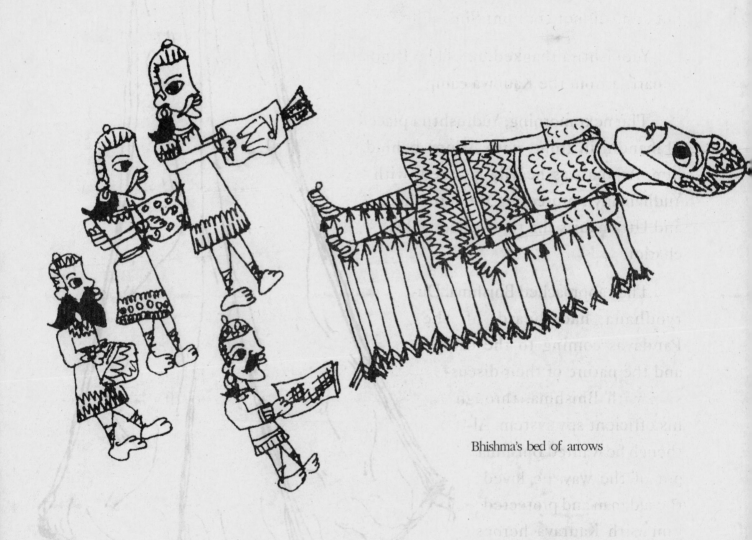

Bhishma's bed of arrows

Bhishma heard his mother Ganga's voice, and the voice of the Vasus*, his brothers, beckoning him to come. "Come!" they said, "Join us here, in heaven. Your work on earth is over. Come, Bhishma, come."

72

Bhishma closed his eyes and listened to these voices for a few minutes. He then remembered his duty to Duryodhana. His eyes blazed, as he sent arrows in all directions. Thousands of Pandavas troops reached Yama's court that day.

Finally, Arjuna put an end to Bhishma's merciless slaughter. He covered the mighty warrior in arrows. Tired, Bhishma fell down and the arrows propped him up. "Ha, ha!" he said, "I am on a bed of arrows, a fit bed for a kshatriya."

Bhishma's head dropped down and he asked for a cushion. Thousands of kings rushed to their camps and returned with cushions of all shapes, sizes and colour. But Bhishma nodded them all away. "Give me a pillow fit for a kshatriya," said Bhishma. Arjuna nodded and sent four arrows flying. The arrowheads propped Bhishma's head up.

"I am feeling thirsty, my son," Bhishma said. Arjuna raised his bow and released an arrow. It struck the ground with such force that water sprang up. Bhishma's mouth was full of sweet water. He lay on his bed of arrows and looked at the sky.

The gods in heaven wondered whether Bhishma was dying now, for the sun was in the northern sector and it was an inauspicious time to die. Bhishma smiled, as if he read their thoughts. He remembered his father's words from more than half a century ago. "You can choose the time of your death, son," his father had said.

Yes, he was tired of life and wanted to return to his mother and his brothers, but he could not die now. It was against his Dharma. He would die when the sun was in a more auspicious sector.

Bhishma watched the sunset and then closed his eyes.

Chapter 26
Commander-in-Chief Drona

Drona takes over

On the dawn of the eleventh day, Duryodhana faced the difficult task of choosing a new commander. "Help me Karna," he said. He was desperate. "There are so many great heroes here and if I were to choose one, I would offend the rest." "Hmm..." thought Karna. Finally, he said, "Why not choose Drona? He is the greatest among all the heroes here and nobody will be offended if he is chosen."

Duryodhana liked Karna's idea and immediately asked Drona to be his commander-in-chief. Drona liked the humble manner in which Duryodhana asked him and agreed.

The coronation of the commander-in-chief was performed quickly. Drona, still overwhelmed by Duryodhana's request, granted him a boon. "I want Yudhishtira captured alive," Duryodhana said. Drona replied "If you can lure Arjuna away, it shall be done."

The Pandava spies duly reported this and Arjuna burned in anger when he heard of Drona's promise.

Drona arranged his army in the formidable Sakata Vyuha* formation. In response, Dhrishtadyumna quickly arranged his troops in the Krauncha* formation. Karna was placed in front of the Sakata Vyuha. On seeing him, the Kaurava army raised loud cheers.

When Arjuna was out of sight, Drona attempted to catch Yudhishtira. But first he had to defeat formidable foes such as Satyajit, Satyaki, Dhrishtadyumna and Shikandin. When he was on the verge of capturing Yudhishtira, Arjuna was seen. Krishna was driving the chariot madly and Arjuna's arrows flew, killing thousands of Kaurava troops. Arjuna and Drona came face to face. Red with wrath, Arjuna defeated Drona, his teacher. Altogether the day was with the Pandavas. There had been many grand duels that day.

Arjuna's arrows

Chapter 27
The Samsaptakas

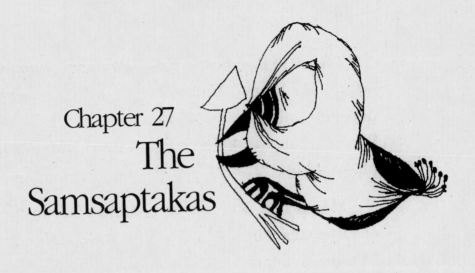

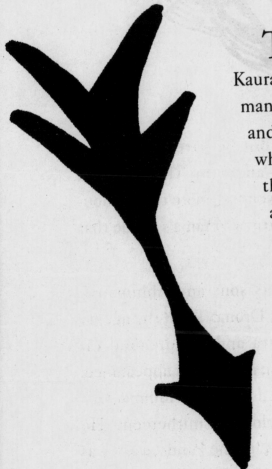

That night, there was a council of war held in the Kaurava camp. Duryodhana, as usual, blamed his commander. Drona was angered by Duryodhana's words and said, "I nearly captured Yudhishtira today, but when I was about to capture him, Arjuna came on the scene. As I said before, if you want Yudhishtira alive, you must lure away Arjuna from his side."

Then Susharma, the Trigarta king said, "I and my Samsaptaka* army have sworn to accomplish any mission we undertake successfully. Or else we die. I will challenge Arjuna tomorrow. If he does not accept the challenge, he will have to acknowledge that we are superior to him. He knows that. Therefore he cannot refuse this challenge."

77

The next day, Susharma challenged Arjuna who, of course, could not refuse. He begged Yudhishtira's pardon for leaving his side. He said he hoped to finish the Trigartas quickly. But the Samsaptakas had other plans. When Arjuna had killed most of them, the remaining few came back and plagued him.

Meanwhile, Yudhishtira had been left in the care of Satyajit, brother of Draupada. Drona came on to attack Yudhishtira, but had to first fight Dhrishtadyumna. Durmukha, one of the Kaurava brothers, challenged Dhrishtadyumna. The Pandava commander could not refuse. Drona killed Satyajit, Virata's brother Sataanika, and Draupada's other brother, Vrika. The Pandava army was shaken to see the three great heroes die thus, in almost a minute.

However, Drona could not reach Yudhishtira's chariot.

But he gave full vent to his anger on the Pandava army, sending more than a thousand warriors to Yama's abode that day.

Draupadi's sons and Abhimanyu fought back at Drona. Then the ageing king Bhagadatta and his dreaded elephant Supritika, made their appearance. Supritika smashed Bhima's, Abhimanyu's and Satyaki's chariots to smithereens. He did as much damage to the Pandava army as a whole division would have done. The Pandavas

78

were ashamed to think that they were fighting against a single elephant and his owner.

Arjuna finished the Samsaptakas by invoking the Vajra, the weapon of his father, Indra. Then there was an awesome fight between Arjuna and Bhagadatta. Bhagadatta invoked the Vaishnava astra, the great astra of Vishnu. Whoever had this astra was immune to any other weapon, as long as it stayed with him. The astra did not harm Arjuna. However, Bhagadatta and his elephant lost their immunity once the astra was released.

Arjuna aimed one arrow at Supritika's chest and released it. The arrow was true to its mark. The great elephant fell down and died. Bhagadatta was Arjuna's next victim. He died in the same way as his elephant.

Thus ended the twelfth day of the war. There were losses on both sides.

Supritika the elephant

Chapter 28
The Young Boy

The next day the remainder of the Trigartas, now joined by a section of Kaurava troops, once again challenged Arjuna. Arjuna, though irritated, could not refuse and the Trigartas drew him away to another part of the battlefield.

Drona arranged his army in the impenetrable Chakra Vyuha*. The Pandavas gasped when they saw this, for only Arjuna in their army could penetrate it. Yudhishtira was in a serious dilemma, for if he did not make a breach in the Vyuha, his troops, who were already being killed in immense numbers, would be vanquished.

Then Abhimanyu came forward. "When I was in my mother's womb," he said, "one night, my father explained to my mother how to breach the Chakra Vyuha. I heard all of it. But my father didn't explain how to come out of the Vyuha. I can make a breach but I can't come out."

Yudhishtira said, "Don't worry, my son, we will hold the breach open." Abhimanyu's handsome face relaxed.

They proceeded to the Chakra Vyuha where Abhimanyu made a breach. The Pandavas dutifully followed and kept the breach open. Everything went well. Then they came to the second layer which consisted of Jayadratha, the Sindhu king, and his army. Abhimanyu went forward. But Jayadratha blocked the Pandavas' path. Long ago, Jayadratha had been humiliated by the Pandavas. He wanted revenge. He went into penance for one year. Lord Shiva, pleased with his devotion, granted him a boon that he would defeat the Pandavas at least once. Now Shiva's boon was being fulfilled. The Pandavas attacked Jayadratha, who defeated them.

Abhimanyu

Meanwhile, Abhimanyu fought on bravely. But the great warriors, Drona, Kripa, Ashwathama, Dushasana's son Laxman, Karna and Kritavarma attacked Abhimanyu. They cut all his bows and killed his charioteer and horses. Abhimanyu jumped out of his chariot, his sword in hand. Drona cut the sword blade from the hilt.

In desperation, Abhimanyu picked up his chariot wheel. But the six warriors split the wheel into a hundred fragments.

Abhimanyu picked up a mace. Dushasana's son Laxman attacked him. They fought hard. Both were tired. Both fainted. Laxman rose first. Just as Abhimanyu was rising, Laxman swung his mace. In one stroke, Abhimanyu was killed. Happy that Abhimanyu was now dead, the warriors danced around the body, just as vultures circle their prey. Six warriors were happy that a sixteen year old boy had died through their efforts. They felt no remorse or shame. They only rejoiced.

The warriors dance

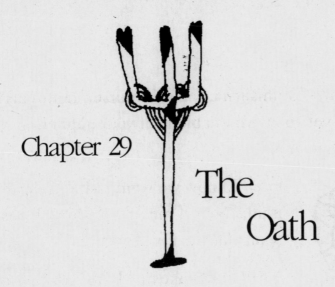

Chapter 29

The Oath

Arjuna and Krishna returned to the camp late. They were greeted by a silent and lonely camp.

As they hurried to the tent of the Pandavas, they encountered sad soldiers who, upon seeing the two cousins, burst into tears.

Wondering why there was so much sadness in the Pandava camp, Krishna and Arjuna opened the tent flap. There again, they were confronted by sad faces. Looking at these faces, Arjuna suddenly became anxious. Then he realised that his son, Abhimanyu, had not wished him as usual. For he would rush out to greet his father everyday. He looked at the faces of his brothers and turned to them, one by one. No one would speak to him. Finally Sahadeva spoke. "Arjuna, your son Abhimanyu died today. We were foolish enough to send him into the Chakra Vyuha. He was killed by Drona, Karna, Ashwathama, Kripa, Kritavarma and Dushasana's son Laxman. But he died an honourable death."

Arjuna was seething with anger. "You, you! My own brothers are responsible for the death of my son. You were aware he only knew how to enter the Chakra Vyuha. How could you send a boy of sixteen in there?

You, Yudhishtira, you call yourself righteous and yet you have the blood of your nephew on your hands."

"I know we were rash," Yudhishtira said, "So kill me, if you think I was responsible for his death."

Bhima broke in, "It's partly our fault, yes. But it's more Jayadratha's fault. He blocked the breach Abhimanyu had made and would not let us enter. So the poor boy was stuck inside, not knowing how to come out."

All the anger Arjuna had towards his brothers was directed at Jayadratha now. "I swear to kill that murderer Jayadratha tomorrow," he said, "and avenge the death of my son Abhimanyu. If not, I will kill myself."

Krishna and Subadra

Arjuna and Krishna left the tent to go and console Subadra and Uttara. On the way Krishna said, "That was very rash of you. For the Kaurava spies have heard your oath. They will protect Jayadratha tomorrow. You might not be able to kill him and then you will lose the war."

Back in the Kaurava camp, Jayadratha was scared. He thought of leaving and returning to his kingdom. But Duryodhana laughed and promised to save Jayadratha.

Arjuna and Krishna consoled the weeping Subadra, and Uttara, who was carrying Abhimanyu's child.

Arjuna consoles Uttara

84

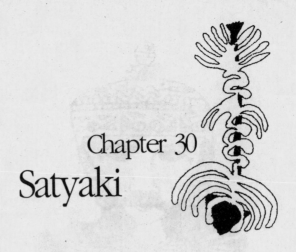

Chapter 30
Satyaki

Varuna's mace

The next morning, Drona arranged his army in a triple Vyuha. Arjuna prepared himself to carry out his oath. But it proved no easy task. First, he fought a duel with Drona. But time was running out fast. So he left the battle unfinished, accepting defeat for the moment, at the hands of his teacher. Next, Arjuna's friend, Kritavarma, fought a tough duel with him. But Kritavarma was soon exhausted.

The next to attack Arjuna was King Srutayudha, who was killed easily. He possessed a mace given by Varuna, which was always accurate to its mark. However, if it was thrown towards an unarmed man, the mace would turn back and kill its thrower. Such was the mace of Srutayudha. In a fit of anger, he threw the mace at Krishna

Varuna

who was unarmed, being a charioteer. The mace, now thrown towards an unarmed man, turned back, hit Srutayudha, and killed him.

Sudakshina, king of the Kambojas, was angered by this sight. He encountered Arjuna, who killed him by piercing his heart with a sharp arrow.

Next Arjuna faced the brothers, Srutayus and Achutayas. They attacked Arjuna furiously. But he killed them effortlessly with the Aindra astra.

Now Arjuna had reached the second Vyuha. Yudhishtira could not see the ape banner of Arjuna. Worried, he sent Satyaki, his protector, to look for Arjuna.

Satyaki was unwilling to leave Yudhishtira's side and expose him to Drona, who had promised to capture him alive. However, on Yudhishtira's persuasion, Satyaki relented.

It was easy to go through the first Vyuha, since Arjuna had already destroyed it. Satyaki fought a duel with Drona. Finding it impossible to defeat Drona, Satyaki did what

86

his teacher Arjuna had done. He gave up the battle, circled around Drona, offering his respects to the great warrior and moved on. A furious Drona followed Satyaki. But now well ahead, Satyaki routed Karna's army as well and went on to encounter Jalasandha, king of the South. He killed Jalasandha with three arrows, cutting his arms and head.

Satyaki went forward to meet his cousin Kritavarma. A furious battle raged between the two. Kritavarma shot Satyaki's charioteer, causing him to faint. Undeterred from the battle and all the more angry, Satyaki seized the reins of his horses in one of his hands and continued to fight with the other. He finally managed to defeat Kritavarma and continued onward.

But by this time, the enraged Drona had caught up with Satyaki. Annoyed, Satyaki shot Drona's charioteer and wounded his horses. The horses bolted around the battlefield in agony, dragging Drona's chariot behind them. Having pacified his horses, Drona returned to his post at the

Kritavarma and Satyaki

entrance of the Vyuha to protect it from further attack from the Pandavas.

Satyaki continued to charge through the ranks. He destroyed the Kaurava army as a mongoose kills a multitude of snakes. He rode forward like an avenging lion. The day was clearly Satyaki's. The Kauravas had never seen this side of Satyaki. They were amazed by his prowess.

Meanwhile Yudhishtira had sent Bhima into the Vyuha to aid Arjuna. Bhima was stopped by Karna and they had a duel. For a time, Bhima seemed to have the upper hand. He cut the strings of Karna's bows and shattered his chariot time and again. On seeing Karna's plight, Duryodhana sent his brothers to help his friend. A smile emerged on Bhima's face as he joyously killed the sons of Dhritarashtra. He killed nine Kauravas. He took great joy in this, for he was completing the oath he had taken nearly fourteen years ago. Only when he killed Vikarna, did he feel remorse for killing the only Kaurava who had objected to the disrobing of Draupadi.

On seeing the deaths of his friend's brothers, Karna fainted. But he soon recovered consciousness and returned to his position on the field. This time Karna defeated Bhima, but remembering his promise to Kunthi, he sought his revenge by merely insulting Bhima.

"Your place is in the kitchen," said Karna with his charming smile, which was now a source of irritation for Bhima. "You should be preparing meals for Virata."

Seeing the manner in which Bhima was being taunted, Arjuna prepared to finish Karna once and for all. But an arrow sent by Ashwathama, diverted his attention and he turned to confront his guru's son.

Arjuna attacked Ashwathama. Satyaki, meanwhile, was challenged by Bhoorisravas. There was an age-old enmity between Satyaki and Bhoorisravas. A long time ago, Sini, Satyaki's grandfather, had gone for the swayamvara of Devaki, Krishna's mother. Having obtained her for his friend and cousin Vasudeva, he left. But a Kuru king called Somadatta obstructed his path.

In the ensuing fight, Sini defeated Somadatta. Sini seized Somadatta by his hair, and placed a foot upon his chest. Somadatta was greatly angered by this and was granted a boon that one of his sons would do the same to one of Sini's descendants.

In the heat of the battle, this old rivalry once again surfaced. Exhausted by his achievements, Satyaki was in no shape for another fight that day. Bhoorisravas took advantage of this situation and very soon cornered Satyaki, who fainted, on account of sheer exhaustion. Bhoorisravas did the very same thing Sini had done to Somadatta many years ago. He placed his foot on Satyaki's chest, and grabbed him by his hair. He was about to slay Satyaki, when Arjuna intervened and cut off Bhoorisravas' right arm. "I am sorry," Arjuna apologised, "but you were about to kill my friend in an unjust and cruel manner." The aged warrior acknowledged this with a wave of his remaining arm.

Bhoorisravas made preparations to abandon this world. He spread kusha grass on the ground and sat in meditation. He was going to leave his body by yoga. Suddenly Satyaki sprang up, seized Bhoorisravas by the head and with one stroke of his sword, killed him. Arjuna was angry with Satyaki for having killed Bhoorisravas, when he had surrendered. This was the one and only incident that marred Satyaki's otherwise pure life.

Chapter 31
The Trick

Jayadratha rejoicing

The sun was slowly but steadily going down the horizon. Krishna pointed it out to Arjuna. "Look," he said, "the sun is setting, Arjuna, you must act fast if you want to complete your oath and avenge Abhimanyu's death."

91

On Krishna's words of advice, Arjuna approached Jayadratha directly. But a great force of warriors was protecting the Sindhu king. Arjuna made quick work of the warriors, but the sun would surely set by the time they were all vanquished.

Krishna devised a brilliant plan. He covered the sun with his discus, making it appear as if night had fallen. The whole Kaurava army looked upwards. Karna, Drona and the king rejoiced, thinking they had carried off their coup. But alas, that was not the case. For as soon as Jayadratha had turned his glad eyes towards his supposed saviour, the sun, Arjuna sent a shaft which sliced Jayadratha's head completely off.

Jayadratha's head

Krishna told Arjuna to direct the arrow towards the Samantapanchaka forest, where Jayadratha's father was performing his evening prayers. Arjuna did so. The head alighted on the old king's lap. After finishing his prayers, the king, oblivious of the head lying on his lap, arose. The head tumbled down, and the moment it touched the ground, Jayadratha's father's head exploded. As the amazed onlookers watched, Krishna recalled his divine discus and the sun shone for a few minutes in its final glory, before really setting this time.

Chapter 32
The Night Battle

Returning to the Pandava front, Arjuna asked the reason for this strange event. Krishna answered, "A long time ago, Jayadratha's father was granted a boon. If a person caused Jayadratha's head to fall on the ground, that person's head would explode into a thousand fragments. And that is the reason why I asked you to direct the head towards the forest. Since Jayadratha's father caused his head to fall, he died."

Duryodhana was extremely unhappy. He reprimanded Drona for allowing Arjuna and Satyaki into the Vyuha. Drona took a great oath that he would not remove his armour until he killed all of Duryodhana's enemies.

There was an intense battle between Duryodhana and Yudhishtira. They seemed to be bent on destroying each other. Nobody had ever seen them fight so magnificently before. In the heat of the battle, they could be easily mistaken for Karna and Arjuna. Drona interfered in the duel and made the fight

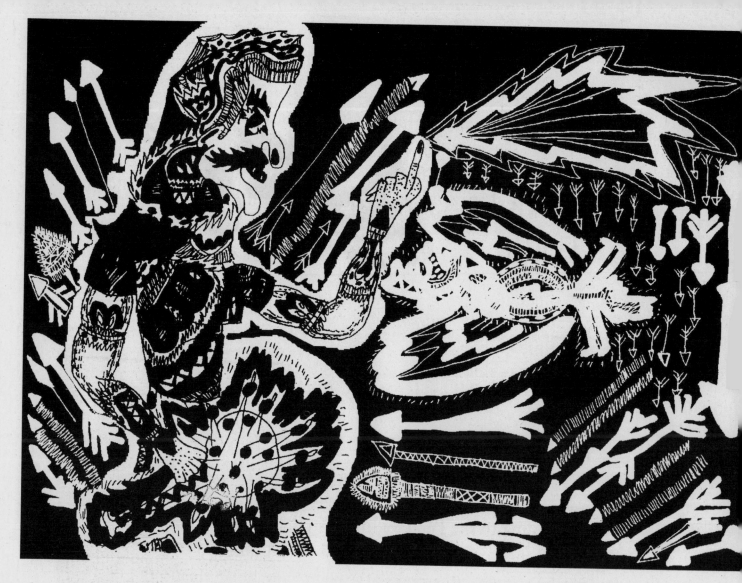

Gatotkacha's maya tactics

general, once again. But as the night grew on, so did the darkness. Yet Drona fought with renewed energy. He seemed to be making short work of the Pandava army.

Bhima also seemed to be bent on destroying, for he eliminated a great number of Kauravas that night.

Gatotkacha, Bhima's demon son, was also causing great havoc. He and his band of asuras were using maya tactics, as their power increased a ten-fold at night. Duryodhana was unhappy when he saw the demons wipe out his exhausted army. Ashwathama, on seeing his friend's distress, boldly went forward to suppress Gatotkacha. Gatotkacha tried to impress Ashwathama by using his magical powers. However, his attempts proved to be useless. Ashwathama did not turn a hair when he saw the amazing things Gatotkacha could do with his extraordinary powers. Seeing that maya was useless, Gatotkacha fought with Ashwathama with a bow and arrow. When things got a little difficult for the demon, Gatotkacha once again resorted to maya tactics. But this time Ashwathama got the better of him, and Gatotkacha fainted.

Meanwhile, Shakuni went to the Pandava front to confront the Pandavas there. Bhima and the great war veteran, Baahlika, were fighting each other. Baahlika was a very ancient Kuru monarch who was even older than Bhishma. Today, he had lost his grandsons Sala and Bhoorisravas. He was on the warpath now. Though a very old man, Baahlika was made of tough material. Now, possessed with anger, he fought fiercely. An exhausted Bhima finally killed him with a powerful mace.

Baahlika

Ashwathama and Dhrishtadyumna were locked in a duel. Each seemed intent on killing the other. Ashwathama thought he could save his father from his fate by killing Dhrishtadyumna.

Dhrishtadyumna wanted to finish both father and son. But they exchanged more insults than blows. Eventually, Ashwathama managed to defeat Dhrishtadyumna by cutting his bow and shattering his chariot.

Yudhishtira had a fight with Duryodhana. In an attempt to save Yudhishtira, Bhima challenged Duryodhana in such a way that he could not refuse. Drona joined the general fight against Yudhishtira. He sent the Vayu astra after the oldest Pandava. But Yudhishtira met it with the same astra. Krishna then advised Yudhishtira to forget Drona and to challenge Duryodhana instead.

Chapter 33
Revenge

It was very dark. The soldiers mistook their comrades for the enemy. To avoid this, Drona ordered his soldiers to carry torches. The Pandavas did the same. The battlefield was illuminated by the brilliance of the torches. There were magnificent fights between individuals. There was no screech of arrows, no chanting of mantras as astras were released, no furious battle cries or the sound of chariot wheels sinking into the earth, to disturb the warriors.

There was a duel between Karna and Sahadeva. Sahadeva flung a mace at Karna. But Karna warded it off with great ease. Weaponless, Sahadeva did the only thing open to him. He grabbed his chariot wheel and hurtled it

The son of Jatasura

towards Karna with great force. But Karna destroyed it with a single arrow. Now Sahadeva was at the mercy of Karna. "This is it." he thought, "Karna will surely kill me now."

But Karna remembered the promise he had made to Kunthi. He touched Sahadeva with the tip of his bow and said, "Fight with your equals, boy! Why don't you join your brother Arjuna at the front? He is a warrior superior to you." The dazed Sahadeva left, wondering why Karna had not killed him.

Meanwhile Satyaki had killed yet another king, who was called Bhoori. Bhima had defeated Duryodhana. Gatotkacha was ferocious. He and his band of asuras were wiping out the Kauravas. Worried, Duryodhana sent Karna to counter Gatotkacha. There was a furious fight between the two. The son of the asura Jatasura, whom Gatotkacha had killed earlier, came to Duryodhana, offering his services to avenge his father's death. Duryodhana accepted his help. The son of Jatasura relieved Karna.

The two demons used maya tactics. Jatasura's son was fierce. He and his band of demons began to make short work of the Pandava army. Gatotkacha and Jatasura's son fought a duel. But Jatasura's son soon lost his chariot. He engaged Gatotkacha in hand to hand combat. The fight went on for a long time. Gatotkacha decided that his opponent had lived long enough. He leapt up into the sky and flew down, gaining speed. With a sweep of his sword, he cut off the head of Jatasura's son. The body crumpled and he fell to the ground lifeless.

Gatotkacha carried the head to Duryodhana's chariot. He said with a sneer, "Tradition says that you should never visit a king without a gift. O King, this is my gift to you." And he placed the head in the chariot. Duryodhana quaked in fear.

Gatotkacha

At that moment an asura named Alayudha approached Duryodhana. He said, "Bhima killed all my relatives—Baka, Kirmira, and Hidimba. Now I want my revenge by killing his son and then him."

Alayudha's entry into the battle could not have been better timed. Duryodhana gratefully accepted his help. At that time Gatotkacha was fighting with Karna. He fought with Alayudha for a short time. Bhima came to his son's help and accosted Alayudha. Gatotkacha turned his back on his uncle Hidimba's avenger and resumed his battle with Karna.

Meanwhile Alayudha's army caused great havoc in the Pandava ranks. Bhima was giving in slowly to Alayudha. On seeing Bhima in a dire situation, the Pandavas requested Gatotkacha to help his father. Gatotkacha left Karna. The Pandavas now engaged Karna in a general fight. Gatotkacha swooped down, like he had done before, and cut off Alayudha's head.

Chapter 34
Gatotkacha and the Indra Astra

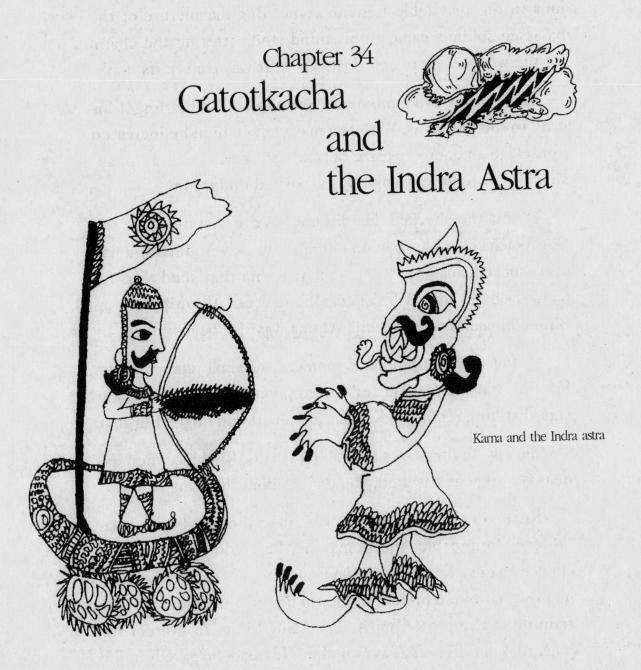

Karna and the Indra astra

Karna and Gatotkacha resumed their interrupted battle. Gatotkacha was up to his tricks once more. He cleverly dodged Karna's astras by either assuming a different form or by countering them with his maya. Around Karna were the desperate Kaurava soldiers, impaled by Gatotkacha's troop of demons. "Save us, Karna," were their dying words, "Use Indra's astra."

Karna bit his lip. He wanted to use the astra against Arjuna in the inevitable fight to come. But the picture of the harassed soldiers came to his mind, and, uttering the charm for the weapon, he released the astra. It was true to its mark.

Even in his dying moment, Gatotkacha did not forget his duty to the Pandavas. With the maya left in him, he increased himself to an enormous size before hitting the ground. An akshauhini of Kaurava troops was squashed under him.

Bhima was shocked. He did not believe that his brave son Gatotkacha could have been killed so quickly. Yudhishtira was also shocked, absolutely shocked. Together they shed tears for Gatotkacha, who had finished off the asura Alayudha, whom Bhima himself could not kill. Arjuna was also heartbroken.

But at this inappropriate moment, Krishna jumped down from his chariot and started dancing with joy. The Pandavas stared at him, repulsed. Krishna ran about and hugged Arjuna.

Finally Yudhishtira said, "What is this, Krishna, when our dear Gatotkacha has died, you dance about, hugging Arjuna?"

Krishna replied, "I knew ever since the war began, that however formidable Arjuna may be, he could never stand a chance against Karna. Karna had not only his earrings and armour which would protect him from death, but he also had the training of the great Parashurama. But Indra, to protect Arjuna, took the armour away from him. Instead, he gave him the Indra astra, a weapon that could have easily killed Arjuna. But Indra also told him that he could use it only once. Now since he has used it against Gatotkacha, he can never harm Arjuna."

The Pandavas found little solace in this. They still mourned the loss of Gatotkacha. Yudhishtira, enraged with Karna for killing Gatotkacha, charged towards him. But Vyasa intervened and told Yudishthira to return to the ranks of his army.

Krishna leaping with joy

103

Chapter 35
The Death
of the
Brahmin

Ashwathama the elephant

The soldiers were very tired. They had been fighting since dawn. Most of them were falling asleep. Arjuna realised the miserable condition the troops were in. He proposed to Duryodhana that the two armies sleep now and resume the battle when they awoke. His proposal was accepted. The soldiers fell asleep where they stood.

One fourth of the night remained, when both the armies awoke. The battlefield was filled with the sounds of soldiers preparing themselves for battle. The fighting began in a short while. By and by, the sun arose from his slumber and relieved the moon. There was a tinge of red in the sky, as if there had been fighting there too and the blood of the soldiers had stained the sky.

Every man welcomed the warm rays of the sun.

The fighting began with renewed strength. Duryodhana once again harassed Drona. He accused him of being partial to the Pandavas. Drona was very irritated with Duryodhana. The vision of his entire life flooded his mind. It was not a life which any man would be proud of. Exasperated, he turned away from Duryodhana. He was fed up with the war. He turned his attention to the army, and divided it into two, the left and right divisions.

Krishna took Arjuna's chariot towards the left wing. He fought with four great Kaurava heroes. They did not stand a chance against Arjuna.

Meanwhile, Drona fought in the northern sector of the battlefield. He fought with the three sons of Dhrishtadyumna. He killed them quickly. Draupada, who saw his grandsons killed before his very eyes, rushed headlong towards Drona. He prepared to avenge the deaths of his grandsons. Virata came to Draupada's help. But they proved to be no match for the brahmin. In a short time they themselves reached Yama's abode. Dhrishtadyumna howled with rage when he saw this. He took a great oath, as he charged towards Drona. "I swear", he said "that I will see Drona killed before this day ends. I promise to fulfil the purpose for which I have been born."

As soon as the Pandavas heard the oath, they rushed to help Dhrishtadyumna. The Kauravas likewise protected Drona. Neither the Pandavas nor Dhrishtadyumna could get at Drona.

Then Bhima hit upon a brilliant plan. "The only way to kill Drona is to tell him that his son Ashwathama is dead," he said. The Pandavas did not like the plan, but it was the only practical solution. So Bhima killed an elephant called Ashwathama.

Shamefaced, he approached Drona and said, "Revered Teacher, Ashwathama is dead." At first Drona did not realise the weight of these words of Bhima. During the time that elapsed between his hearing of the words and understanding their importance, he sent twenty four thousand soldiers to their death. Then finally, the news penetrated. He was shocked. He could not believe that his son Ashwathama could be killed.

Unseen to all, except him, the sages of heaven led by Drona's father, Bharadwaja, appeared before him. Bharadwaja said, "Son, it is time you joined us. You have finished your duty." With that the sages disappeared.

Bharadwaja advising Drona

In desperation, Drona asked Yudhishtira. "Yudhishtira, you never lie. Tell me the truth. Is my son Ashwathama really dead?"

Yudhishtira gulped. He had known this question was coming, but had hoped it would not. In a meek voice he said, "Yes, Ashwathama is dead." He added in a whisper which no one could hear, "Ashwathama, the elephant." Until now, Yudhishtira had not uttered a single lie. Now that he had done so, his chariot which had always remained four inches above the

106

Yudhishtira and Arjuna

ground, became level with all the other chariots. His righteous Dharma had been keeping his chariot aloft, until the moment he uttered that one falsehood.

Drona broke down. His son was dead. Yes, those sages had been right when they had told him to join them. He assumed a yogic posture and prepared to leave his body. Dhrishtadyumna seized this opportunity to avenge the deaths of his brothers, sons and father.

Moving fast, he cut off Drona's head with his sword, ignoring the pleas of Arjuna to spare the great teacher.

Then there was a shining light, as the spirit of Drona assumed its rightful place in heaven. Only Kripa, Yudhishtira and Krishna, apart from Sanjaya, witnessed this.

The slaying of Drona

Chapter 36
Astras

Just at that moment, Ashwathama heard about his father's death from his uncle, Kripa. Enraged at the manner in which his father died, he seized his bow and brought new courage into the hearts of the Kaurava army. He led them forward to the battlefield.

The Pandavas saw him coming, with anger on his brow. They heard the great oath he took, to kill the murderers of his father, Yudhishtira and Dhrishtadyumna.

Arjuna, looking at the son of the great Drona advancing, said, "Ashwathama is coming to avenge his father's death. He will surely kill us with the anger inside him. I tried to prevent you, Dhrishtadyumna, from killing him and now you are going to reap the fruits of your sin." He turned around to face Dhrishtadyumna and Yudhishtira. "I think," he continued, "that anything is better than killing the man who has been like a father to us. We should have remained in the forest. Now we have caused so much grief and sadness not only to others, but to ourselves as well."

The Pandavas and their friends gathered in the tent were silent for a moment. Then Dhrishtadyumna broke the silence. "I killed Drona, yes.

Bhima and Satyaki

But by doing so, I have prevented the deaths of thousands of men who would have died at his hands. I killed him sinfully. But the methods you used for killing Jayadratha were not righteous."

Satyaki was filled with anger when he heard these insults being hurled at Arjuna. "How dare you insult my teacher in such a manner! You, whose hands are stained with the blood of the sinful killing of Drona." Dhrishtadyumna replied, "Yes, yes, look who's talking. Why don't you first think of the manner in which you killed Bhoorisravas? Wasn't that just as sinful as you claim my killing of Drona to be?" Satyaki rushed towards Dhrishtadyumna, mace in hand, ready to kill him. Bhima jumped on to Satyaki, dragging him away, and thus prevented the murder of Dhrishtadyumna.

Sahadeva, the peacemaker among the Pandavas, said to the two, "You are both vital to us in this war. So please let us put the death of Drona behind us and face Ashwathama."

Just then Ashwathama let loose the Narayana astra, one of the most deadly astras. The whole sky was bombarded with shining discuses, and weapons of all sorts. To avoid the oncoming danger, the Pandava army threw themselves onto the ground. Duryodhana was pleased with Ashwathama's success. He asked him to send the astra again. But Ashwathama replied that the astra could not be recalled.

Agni astra

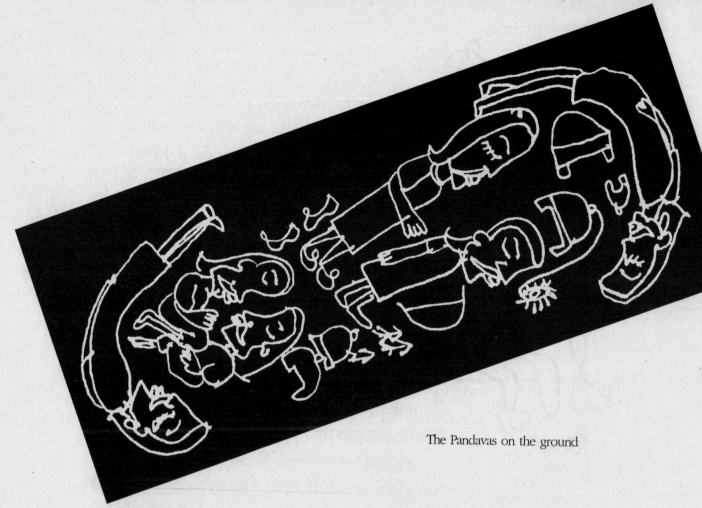

The Pandavas on the ground

Spotting Dhrishtadyumna among the mass of soldiers, Ashwathama leapt to complete his oath. There was a fierce battle between the two. But the advantage was clearly Ashwathama's. Arjuna, seeing Dhrishtadyumna in the powerful grasp of the angry Ashwathama, came to the former's help. He challenged Ashwathama. Ashwathama could not refuse.

The fight lasted for a long time. Ashwathama wanted to resume his fight with his father's killer. So, he sent the Agni astra towards Arjuna. The Pandava army was burnt in agony under the fury of the Agni astra. Arjuna sent the Brahma astra to counter the Agni astra. The conflict ended. But Ashwathama was shocked to see his astras destroyed so easily. Later, he met Vyasa and asked him the reason for the failure of the astras. "This is because you sent the astras against Arjuna and Krishna, the incarnations of Nara and Narayana. These divine sages, in this birth or any other, cannot be harmed by the astras that belong to them."

The sun set at the end of the fifteenth day of the war.

110

The Brahma astra

Chapter 37
The Sixteenth Day

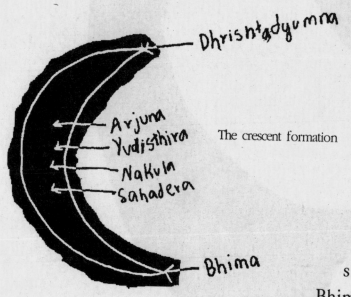

The crescent formation

The next morning, Karna was appointed commander of the Kaurava forces. Compared with the brutal fighting of the day before, the sixteenth day was unnaturally subdued. The Pandava army was formed in the shape of a crescent. One tip had Bhima guarding it and the opposite tip had the commander of the Pandava army, Dhrishtadyumna, guarding it. The centre was made up of Arjuna, Yudhishtira, Nakula and Sahadeva.

Karna had arranged the Kaurava army in the formidable Makara Vyuha*. He himself made up the mouth. Shakuni and his son Uluka made up the eyes. Ashwathama was stationed at the head. Kripa, Kritavarma, Sushena (one of Karna's sons) and Shalya made up the legs. The Kaurava brothers made up the neck and the tail.

Karna and the twins

There was a duel between Nakula and Karna. Karna defeated Nakula and insulted him in the same way he had insulted Sahadeva, by refusing to kill him. Satyaki killed the Kekaya brothers, who fought on the side of the Kauravas. Bhima killed a king called Kshemadhruthi and met Ashwathama in a duel.

So the sixteenth day of the war ended.

Chapter 38
Shalya
the Charioteer

The seventeenth day dawned. Duryodhana knew that today Karna would meet Arjuna. They had decided last night. So, to ensure the victory of his friend, he requested Shalya to hold the reins of Karna's horses. Shalya was a charioteer, equal to Krishna. At first he was angry. "What! Do you expect me to guide the horses of a suta-putra? It should be the other way around!" But finally Shalya consented to be Karna's charioteer.

Karna and Shalya set out for the battlefield. Karna was fierce and frightening. Meanwhile, Shalya tried to live up to the promise he had made to Yudhishtira when he had been tricked into joining Duryodhana. Thus Shalya made remarks magnifying the greatness of the Pandavas.

Karna's chariot

Shalya the charioteer

Karna felt depressed by Shalya's taunting words. But he knew what Shalya was up to. So he said, "You are doing a good job of frightening me. Yes, I know the Pandavas are great and that today I will meet death at the hands of Arjuna. But today will be my happiest day. If I kill Arjuna, the world will know of me. And if I die, I will die for my friend Duryodhana and gain heaven in the process."

Karna met Yudhishtira and fought with greater vigour. He cut Yudhishtira's bow and then destroyed a javelin sent at him by Yudhishtira with just two arrows. Satyaki, and the other heroes who came to the help of the eldest Pandava were turned back.

Karna cut open Yudhishtira's armour. Blood flowed profusely from Yudhishtira's body. Yet, he sent four more javelins after Karna. But Karna broke all of them and had Yudhishtira at his mercy. Karna could not bear the sight of his brother bleeding. He insulted him much the same way as he insulted Nakula, Sahadeva and Bhima. This was the last insult he hurled at his brothers.

Karna harassed the Pandava army so much that Bhima and the others could not stand this attack. But Bhima had heard the insult thrown at Yudhishtira by Karna. He came towards Karna with anger in his heart. He was more angry than he was on the day Gatotkacha died. Shalya warned Karna of the oncoming danger. But Karna met Bhima with a smile on his lips. Bhima wanted to make Karna pay for insulting Yudhishtira. But Shalya prevented him from doing so.

Yudhishtira and Karna

Karna wanted to continue his fight with his younger brother. Duryodhana realised his intentions and so sent a few of his broth-

116

ers to assist his best friend. Bhima looked as if his favourite dish was being served to him. In no time he killed all of them. Some of the allies of the Pandavas came to help Bhima. The fight became general once more.

Meanwhile, Arjuna was fighting with the Samsaptakas who, since the beginning of the war, had been harassing him. Susharma, the king of the Trigartas, commander of the Samsaptakas, was soon defeated.

Bhima and Karna

Arjuna now had to confront Ashwathama. He finished off Ashwathama with a few astras and injured his horses. In agony, they bolted around the field.

Arjuna next tackled the king of Magada and his brother. In no time at all they both lay dead. In the Pandava lines Karna and Yudhishtira met again in a duel. Karna wounded Yudhishtira so badly, that Yudhishtira had to return to his tent.

Returning to the front, Arjuna did not see his eldest brother. He heard that Yudhishtira had retired to his tent with severe wounds. Yudhishtira was disappointed to see Arjuna return without the blood of the sutaputra Karna on his hands.

This time Arjuna stepped out of the tent with the resolution to kill Karna. Arjuna and Karna moved towards each other, each with the intention of killing the other. Shalya was overcome with admiration for Karna. He was amazed at how Karna rushed headlong to his own death. But to the disappointment of the two enemies, their fight became general.

Chapter 39
Dushasana's Death

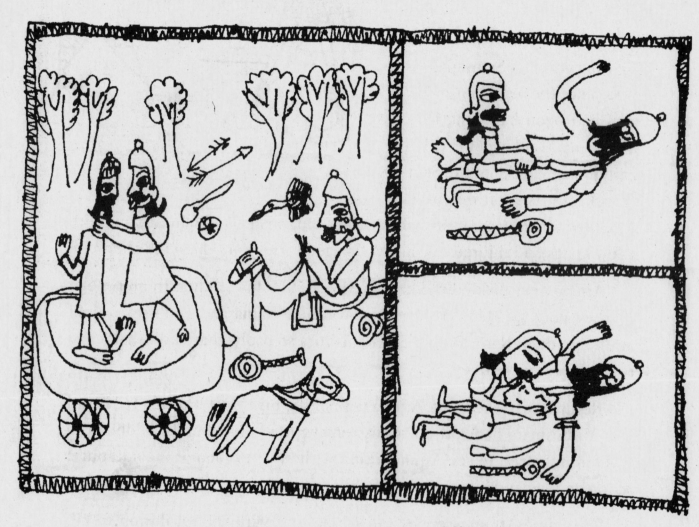

Dushasana and Bhima

There was a duel between Bhima and Dushasana. A conversation was carried out during the duel. Dushasana claimed to remember everything from the time the Pandavas escaped from the house of lac. But he forgot the most crucial detail—Bhima's vow to drink his blood.

Dushasana broke Bhima's bow. Angered by this, Bhima leapt down from his chariot, and with a blow of his mace, killed Dushasana's horses. He climbed into Dushasana's chariot and sent the Kaurava reeling to the ground. He then cut of the hand of his cousin and cried out, "See now, Draupadi's oath is completed. She can see the cut hand of the man who dared to touch her hair. And look, now, as I complete the oath I have taken."

With that, Bhima ripped open the chest of his cousin and drank the blood that gushed out in a stream. The warriors were horrified as they watched this inhuman deed. But Bhima was happy, for he had completed the oath he took years ago, at the end of the dice game.

Draupadi's revenge

Draupadi was sent for. With her hair streaming behind her, she ran to the corpse of Dushasana. She washed her hair in the river of blood that flowed by. Now, she too had completed her oath.

Meanwhile, Karna was stupefied. For, his only surviving son Vrishasena was killed before his very eyes by Arjuna. Tears filled his eyes and ran down his face. He approached Arjuna for the inevitable duel.

Shalya was full of compassion for Karna. He swore, "If you die in this fight Karna, I promise to avenge you or else die in the attempt." Karna was pleased with Shalya's words. But before he could say anything, the chariot of Arjuna approached them.

119

Chapter 40
The
Duel

Agni

The gods in heaven had gathered to see this battle. Surya and Indra nearly fought the battle on behalf of their sons.

At first the battle was gentle. Karna cut the bowstring of the Gandiva. With a smile on his face, Arjuna strung it. Again Karna broke it, but in a moment's time Arjuna had re-strung it. This happened eleven times. Then Arjuna sent his astras after Karna. Karna countered the Agni astra sent by Arjuna with the Varuna astra.

Black clouds filled the sky and thunder rumbled in the distance.

Both the armies looked skywards, expecting rain. But Arjuna blew the clouds away with the Vayu astra. He followed this astra with the Aindra astra, which continuously showered arrows on the enemy army. Karna was enraged by this deed of Arjuna's. In response, he released the deadly Bhargava astra, the astra of Parashurama, given to Karna by the owner himself. The astra destroyed all the arrows sent by the opponent.

Krishna urged Arjuna to send the Brahma astra. Arjuna released it. Arrows rained down like droplets of rain. But the astra did not harm Karna. He sent thousands of arrows at Arjuna. The arrows hurt Arjuna. He, in return, covered up Karna in a shower of arrows.

The Kaurava army was sunk in gloom, thinking that their commander was dead. But Karna shook off the arrows and proved himself a worthy opponent of Arjuna. Yudhishtira heard of the battle and went to see it, so he could crow over Karna's defeat.

Karna sent five snake arrows towards Krishna. Arjuna was angered at this attack on his charioteer. Karna then decided to finish Arjuna, once and for all. He sent his most deadly astra, the Naga astra, towards Arjuna. He thought bitterly of his Shakthi, the Indra astra. He wished he still possessed it. But this was no time for feeling sad. He released the Naga astra. Krishna saw the oncoming missile. He made his horses kneel. The astra missed Arjuna. But it struck his jewelled crown, Kirthi. The crown fell to the ground and broke into a thousand pieces. So powerful was the Naga astra.

Chapter 41
The Chariot Wheel

The Chariot Wheel

On the failure of the Naga astra, a Naga came to the assistance of Karna. It was the snake Ashwasena, son of the Naga, Takshaka. Ashwasena's mother had been killed when Arjuna burnt the forest to build Indraprastha. Now, Ashwasena wanted to avenge his mother's death. So he said to Karna, "You will be able to destroy Arjuna with my help. Let me sit on your arrows, then your victory will be assured." But Karna refused the Naga's help. So Ashwasena raised himself in the air and prepared to strike Arjuna. But Arjuna destroyed the snake in midair.

But at that moment, Karna's chariot wheel sank into the soil. Karna remembered the brahmin's curse of long ago: "When you are fighting your most dangerous enemy, in your most longed for fight, your chariot wheel will sink into the ground." Now it was coming true.

With great effort, he attempted to remember the mantra for the Brahma astra. But Parashurama's curse, that his astras would fail him when he needed them most, was working. Karna then jumped down to pull the sunken chariot wheel. Arjuna sent the Agni astra at him. Once again, Karna destroyed it with the Varuna astra. Even while countering the arrows sent by Arjuna, Karna tried to release his chariot wheel from the strong grip of the earth.

Karna nearly killed Arjuna once. Arjuna fell down with the impact of a powerful arrow sent by Karna. But he recovered, and was all the more angry. By then, Karna was exhausted by his efforts to remember the mantra. He pleaded with Arjuna to give him time to pull out the chariot wheel. Arjuna, a chivalrous fighter, would have granted Karna the extra time. But Krishna reminded Arjuna of the many times Karna had not shown mercy to his opponents.

Karna's smile

Even as Karna tried to lift his chariot wheel, Arjuna sent a sharp arrow to kill him. The Kauravas watched, shocked to see their commander, their only support for the past two days, about to die. Karna turned his head to see the approaching arrow. There was a smile on his face as he died, a smile of infinite happiness and triumph. The arrow cut his head from his body. As his head fell to the ground, the smile was still on Karna's lips. The third commander of the Kauravas was dead.

Chapter 42
Sorrow

Then an amazing thing happened. The sun, in mourning for his dead son, sank at noonday. The sun could not bear the sight of his dead child. The gods in the sky cried out in agony, at Karna's death. The Kaurava army quaked in fear.

The sorrow of the sun

But the Pandava army gave a shout of triumph. Their joy was at odds with the sorrow of the people dear to Karna, the diminishing rays of the sad sun and the unhappy gods. But in the midst of this mourning, Yudhishtira jumped for joy and scrambled into Arjuna's chariot, to see Karna's dead form. There was great rejoicing in the Pandava camp that night .

Duryodhana broke down. He could not believe that his beloved Karna was dead. Shalya consoled him. But it was of no use. With Karna dead, life was empty for Duryodhana. Never had he been so unhappy in his life before. That night, Duryodhana saw the body of the man who had been his best friend. He then went to Bhishma who was still waiting for the sun to move into an auspicious sector. There, Duryodhana broke down once again.

Bhishma felt sorry for his heartbroken grandson. He said, "Karna was not a sutaputra. He was born a kshatriya, and he died the noble death of a kshatriya. He died a death which every man would envy."

Duryodhana learns of Karna's birth

Duryodhana started at these words. He was surprised to know that his friend was a kshatriya. He said, "Grandsire, do you know the woman who ruined Karna's life? Do you know the story of the woman who did this great injustice, the greatest injustice possible, to her son?"

Bhishma replied, "Karna, who was known as Radheya, the son of Radha, was not her son at all. He was actually the son of Kunthi. Kunthi did not want to cause a scandal and she set her baby boy afloat on the river Ganga. Radha and Adhiratha found the baby."

"And tell me, did Karna know of his lineage?" asked Duryodhana.

"Why, yes, he knew. His father, the Sun God, appeared in a dream and told him so. Then, Krishna and Kunthi both told him the secret of his birth and asked him to join his brothers, the Pandavas. But he claimed to be your friend and refused to join his brothers, even if it meant his death. He was loyal to you until the moment he died."

Duryodhana heard the story of the man who gave up all that he could have had, for him. He wept at this story. But he found courage in the greatest tragedy of all. Now he had no fear of dying. He returned to the camp.

Chapter 43
The Prowess of Shalya

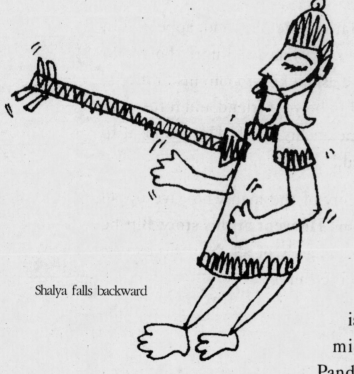

Shalya falls backward

The next morning Shalya was appointed commander of the Kaurava army. He was pleased with the honour Duryodhana had bestowed on him.

Shalya was the most experienced fighter left on the battlefield of Kurukshetra. He organised the scanty Kaurava army in a formidable Vyuha. In response, the Pandavas divided their slightly larger army into three divisions.

The Kauravas decided to have no duels. Only general fights would take place. Shalya fought courageously. He destroyed large numbers of the Pandava army as a river floods a land. Yudhishtira decided that even though Shalya was their uncle, he had to be destroyed. Krishna agreed with him.

Yudhishtira and Shalya met in a fight. Yudhishtira set all other thoughts aside and fixed his mind on just one thought—to kill Shalya. Yudhishtira aimed a powerful javelin embedded with stones towards Shalya's chest. The javelin struck its target.

Shalya fell backwards under the impact of the javelin. He lay on his back, his arms spread out. The great Shalya, uncle of the Pandavas, was now dead.

Seeing their commander dead, the Kaurava troops ran in all directions, trying to save their lives. But Duryodhana rallied his soldiers together. In a voice full of courage, he cried out, "We claim to be kshatriyas. Let us make ourselves worthy of that name. Think of all those brave men who died during the last few days. Let us attain heaven by dying an honourable death on the battlefield."

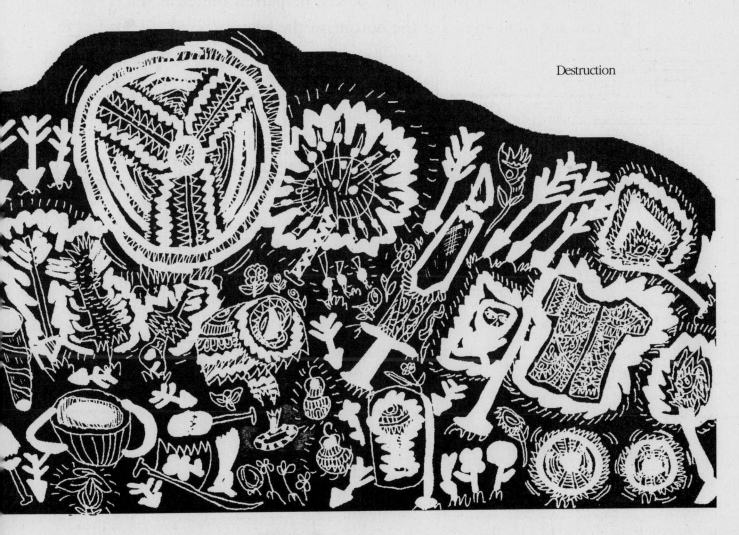

Destruction

All the soldiers listened to the Duryodhana's brave words. Each of them felt a surge of courage. They fought with renewed strength, even though they knew it would be the last time they ever fought.

Shakuni was killed by Sahadeva. Shakuni's son Uluka was killed by Nakula. Both of them fulfilled their oaths. Bhima killed all the remaining Kauravas except Sudarshana and Duryodhana. Then, Sudarshana was also killed.

Now all the soldiers were dead. Duryodhana was sad to see the destruction he had caused because of his foolish whims. But he was tired. He needed rest. There were infinite wounds on his body. He entered a dark cave. There was a small lake gushing there. With his yogic power, he parted the clear waters and went to rest at the bottom of the lake.

Chapter 44
The Fight between Bhima and Duryodhana

Duryodhana submerged

Ashwathama, Kritavarma and Kripa were still alive. They were looking for their king. Sanjaya, who had earlier visited Duryodhana, told them where he was. The three visited Duryodhana and asked him to pick up his mace ."We will continue to fight until we win," said Ashwathama. But Duryodhana was tired and wanted to rest. Several thirsty hunters who had come to drink at the lake heard this interesting conversation. These hunters brought meat for Bhima. Realising that it was Duryodhana in the lake, and knowing that they would be rewarded for their information, they rushed to the camp to give Bhima this valuable piece of news. They got their reward.

Yudhishtira, with the rest of the Pandavas, reached the lake where Duryodhana was submerged. He asked Duryodhana to come out of the lake. But Duryodhana was tired. He said, "Yudhishtira, I am tired of this fighting. Take the earth over which I have ruled so long. Take it. It is not a kingdom worth ruling, filled as it is with the sorrow of widows, the unyielding fields, and the sins of men."

Yudhishtira was angry at these words. He replied, "I have fought for this kingdom for so long. I am not going to accept it as a gift from you. Come out and fight with us."

Duryodhana was humiliated by these words. These were not the words of the gentle Yudhishtira he knew. He rose out of the lake ready to fight. Now, Yudhishtira resumed his kind, gentle attitude. He said, "You may fight with anyone of us, with whatever weapon you want."

Krishna whispered in Yudhishtira's ears, "That was a very bad move of yours. Duryodhana has been practising with a mace on the iron image of Bhima these thirteen years. He is superior to Bhima in the art of the mace. My brother Balarama himself said that."

But Yudhishtira did not heed Krishna's words. Duryodhana chose Bhima and the mace, as Krishna had thought. The two cousins prepared themselves for the duel. At that moment, Balarama entered the cave. He had come to see the duel between his favourite pupil and Bhima.

Krishna was right. Duryodhana was more adept with the mace than Bhima. He cleverly dodged all of Bhima's moves and nearly made Bhima faint. But as Duryodhana leapt into

the air to dodge one of Bhima's moves, Bhima struck Duryodhana beneath the waist and brought him down. This was cheating. But Bhima was happy. Duryodhana's wounds were serious and he would eventually die. Now, Bhima had completed his oath to break Duryodhana's thighs. Balarama was angry to see his pupil struck

Bhima breaking
Duryodhana's thigh

down by unfair means. He raised his weapon, the Plough, to kill all of the Pandavas. But Krishna pacified him. Balarama said, "Duryodhana was felled by foul play. For this you will go to hell, Bhima. Duryodhana will attain heaven, for he died fighting."

With this, Balarama left for Dwaraka. But he was still angry. Duryodhana's eyes filled with tears at the thought that his teacher would have killed the Pandavas for his sake.

The Pandavas left the cave, masters of the entire earth. In the cave they also left the last lord of the earth, the dying Duryodhana.

133

Chapter 45
The Burning of the Camp

Sanjaya came once more to see the king. Duryodhana was touched by his caring. But at the same time, he was approaching his death. He asked Sanjaya to call Ashwathama and the others.

Ashwathama, Kripa and Kritavarma came to see Duryodhana. They were horrified at the amount of pain Duryodhana was going through. Ashwathama was particularly affected by the sight of the dying king. His anger against the Pandavas increased. Duryodhana was pleased by the words of Ashwathama. He asked Kripa to bring water from the lake and anointed Ashwathama as the last commander of the Kaurava forces.

Ashwathama, Kripa and Kritavarma left the presence of the dying king. Ashwathama tried to think of a way to punish the Pandavas. He was suddenly struck by a brilliant idea. He explained his idea to the others. They were flabbergasted at his plan. Kripa said, "That idea is absolutely horrendous. It

isn't at all honourable. Why, if we followed your plan, we would lose every single bit of our dignity."

However, Kripa and Kritavarma had to agree to help Ashwathama. Silently, when the whole camp was asleep, Ashwathama entered the Pandava camp. The Pandavas, as was the custom, had hitched their tents on the border of the battlefield, where the victor was supposed to camp. Ashwathama came into the tent of Dhrishtadyumna. He kicked him awake. Dhrishtadyumna was helpless against Ashwathama who kicked him to death. Then Ashwathama set fire to the camp. Suddenly the whole camp was awake. The sons of Draupadi and the surviving Panchala princes confronted

Ashwathama. Ashwathama killed them all. Kripa and Kritavarma prevented the survivors from escaping.

Draupadi weeps

In the morning the sole survivor of the camp, Dhrishtadyumna's charioteer, narrated to the Pandavas the sad tragedy that had overtaken the camp. Yudhishtira was shocked The Pandavas set off to see the results of the massacre.

Meanwhile Nakula relayed the news to Draupadi. She was heartbroken to see all her sons and brothers dead. She wanted revenge on the person responsible for her grief. To avenge herself, she vowed to get the sacred jewel on Ashwathama's forehead. "It protects the wearer from hunger, thirst and sickness," she said, "I must have it for my revenge." Her husbands swore to get it for her.

136

Chapter 46
The Last Moments
of Duryodhana

The last moments of Duryodhana

A little while earlier, Ashwathama , Kripa and Kritavarma had related the entire proceedings of their victory to Duryodhana. Duryodhana was immensely happy. He said, "Well done, Ashwathama. You have accomplished what all the others could not. You have achieved the goal that I had been striving for all these years. I am very happy with you." With those words Duryodhana died. At that very moment Sanjaya lost the power of seeing the various events that took place on the battlefield of Kurukshetra.

Bhima was very angry with Ashwathama for the deaths of his friend Dhrishtadyumna, and of his sons. With Nakula as his charioteer, Bhima set of to the place where Ashwathama was most likely to be—the forest.

Arjuna and Krishna followed him. On the way Krishna explained to Arjuna that Ashwathama had the Brahmasheersha astra, the same weapon that Drona had rewarded Arjuna, when Arjuna once saved him from a man-eating crocodile. If Krishna was right, Ashwathama would use it now.

Chapter 47
Ashwathama's Jewel

Ashwathama

They caught up with Bhima. In a forest clearing they spotted Ashwathama with a group of sages. Ashwathama also saw them. He still wanted revenge. As Krishna predicted, Ashwathama chanted the incantation for the Brahmasheersha astra. But since Krishna had warned Arjuna, he sent the same astra to counter it. The power of these astras was immense. The moment the astras collided, they could bring about the end of the world. The sages Narada and Vyasa stopped the astras with their yogic powers. They asked Arjuna and Ashwathama to call back the weapons. Arjuna obeyed the sages.

139

But Ashwathama could not do so, for the astra would only obey righteous men. Ashwathama was by no means a righteous man. The astra would not obey him. So he said maliciously, "I cannot call back the astra. It may not kill the Pandavas, but it will kill the descendants of the Pandavas. It will kill the child of Abhimanyu, still in his mother's womb."

Krishna was very angry with Ashwathama for the deeds he had committed. He said, "Your plans are foiled, Ashwathama. For I shall bring that child back to life with these hands of mine. Yes, I shall bring the child back to life."

Since Ashwathama could not recall the astra, the sages ordered him to cut off his priceless jewel, as a punishment. "But," Ashwathama argued, "It keeps the owner safe from hunger, sickness and thirst. I cannot give it to you." Eventually, he was forced to give the jewel to the Pandavas.

Before he left the forest, the sages told him, "You will atone for all the crimes you committed, Ashwathama. You will wander across this earth, shunned by all humanity. No, not even Death will rescue you. You will be immortal. Not a single person will pity you. No, not a single person."

Crestfallen, Ashwathama walked away, to spend his long life in eternal misery.

The Pandavas took the jewel and gave it to Draupadi. She, in turn, gave it to Yudhishtira, who accepted it gratefully.

Chapter 48
The Grief-Stricken Parents

The Pandavas returned to Hastinapura. Their hearts gladdened as they saw the city they had not seen for fourteen years. But ahead of them lay a trying task. They had to see Dhritarashtra. They were not sure how their uncle would react to the deaths of his sons. Not all his sons were dead. Yuyutsu was still alive. But all of the sons borne by Gandhari were dead. They were more afraid of Gandhari, because she had obtained great powers after practising austerities. She might use those powers against them.

The Pandavas first met their uncle. He held out his arms to welcome Bhima.

Dhritarashtra crushing the iron image

141

Gandhari's glance

The Pandava took hesitant steps towards his uncle. Midway, Krishna stopped him and warned him with signs, lest the king should hear. For Dhritarashtra had been practising to crush Bhima. Krishna hurried to the gymnasium from where he brought an iron image of Bhima. Dhritarashtra hugged the image. The force of the hug was so great that the iron image shattered into a hundred fragments. Dhritarashtra realised what he had done and thought he had killed his nephew. But then he realised that Bhima was still alive. This time, he welcomed the Pandava into his arms and did not try to squash him.

Next, they had to meet Gandhari. She was heartbroken, no doubt, but she knew it had been the folly of her son. Since her grief was powerful enough to burn the Pandavas, she turned her head away from them. But her eyes, through her blindfold, caught sight of Yudhishtira's toenails. The toenails of Yudhishtira were burnt.

The rest of the Pandavas were scared of the power of Gandhari. They hid from her. Only when Krishna laughed and told them that they had nothing to fear, did they come out of their hiding places. Yudhishtira meekly left the presence of Gandhari.

Vyasa approached Dhritarashtra and Gandhari. He said, "I have kept the carrion birds, the vultures and the hyenas away with my yogic power. Collect all the wives and relatives of the dead soldiers and let them come and see their dead ones."

Almost at once, women streamed out of the houses and palaces. The rich ones came in their chariot and the poor ones came on foot. They all went to the battlefield and mourned for their sons, husbands and fathers.

Gandhari saw the suffering of these women and pointed it out to Krishna. She said to Krishna, "You have been the cause of the war. Because of your partiality to the Pandavas, you forgot that the Kauravas are also your cousins. Take a good look at the suffering you have caused. See Uttara mourning for Abhimanyu, see the wife of Karna and her daughters-in-law mourning for Karna and his sons. See!"

But on realising that Krishna was still smiling, she said, "You don't care about the amount of pain these women are going through. You just care about your precious Pandavas. I curse you and your clan. In a few years your Yadavas will bring about their own deaths."

Still smiling, Krishna replied, "Thank you, Gandhari. Their destruction was imminent, even before you cursed them. Your curse will enable me to complete my task."

Yudishtira's blackened toenails

Chapter 49
"We have Killed Our Brother!"

Kunthi's revelation

Yudhishtira and the Pandavas stood on the edge of the river Ganga. They were pouring libations to appease the dead. Just a moment ago, Arjuna had poured libations for Abhimanyu. His eyes filled with tears at the memory of his heroic son.

Kunthi remembered the beautiful baby boy that she had abandoned on the river Ganga. His father, Adhiratha had died sometime back and his sons had been killed in the war, so there was no one to appease his soul with offerings. Kunthi decided that she had to do this for the son whom she had neglected all his life. She went up to Yudhishtira and said, "There is someone's soul you still have to appease."

Yudhishtira said, "Who is this, Mother? I have finished offering libations for all the kshatriyas who were killed in the war."

Kunthi swallowed hard and said, "You still have to pour offerings for Karna."

Yudhishtira looked puzzled and said," But Karna was a sutaputra. One of his community must do it for him."

Kunthi replied, "Karna was a kshatriya. You must appease his soul."

The Pandavas were surprised. Was Karna not a sutaputra then, if he was a kshatriya? Meanwhile Krishna stood watching, with a smile on his face. Yudhishtira asked his mother, "Mother, do you know the story of Karna? Please tell it to us."

Kunthi narrated to her sons: "There was this princess once, and she had a beautiful baby boy. You see, at that time, she was unmarried and she feared her father's wrath. So she set the child afloat in the middle of the night on the river Ganga. The charioteer Adhiratha and his wife found him in a box wearing the armour and earrings he was born with. But the princess was always unhappy. Though she had other children, she longed for the little boy whom she had set afloat on the river."

Yudhishtira and his brothers listened, intrigued. Yudhishtira once again asked, "Tell me Mother, who is the mother who wronged her son when he was born?"

Kunthi answered in a choked voice, "The father of Karna was the Sun God and his mother was ... me."

The Pandavas were aghast. "He was our brother! He was our brother! We have killed our brother! And we were so happy to kill him!"

Yudhishtira faced the river and asked his mother, "Did he know this?" Kunthi had already fainted and so Krishna answered, "Yes he knew."

Kunthi fainting

"So you also knew," said Yudhishtira.

"Yes, I did know. But Karna asked me not to tell you," was the reply.

The Pandavas heard the tragic story of the man who could have had the whole world at his feet. But he gave up his birthright, the kingdom that could have been his, for the man who had given him friendship. The Pandavas wept for the sin of killing their brother. They wept for the man who had promised not to kill any of them with the exception of Arjuna.

Chapter 50
Bhishma's Wisdom

Yudhishtira had no wish for the kingdom, after he re-alised he had killed his own brother. But Vyasa coaxed him out of his gloomy state and told him that he had to rule the kingdom. He advised him to go to Bhishma who was still waiting for the sun to move into the northern sector. Bhishma had learnt the secrets of kingship from great teachers such as Brihaspathi and Vasishtha. His mother had reared him to be a king. All that knowledge that Bhishma had learnt should not go to waste. Yudhishtira followed Vyasa's advice and visited Bhishma who imparted to him the secrets of how to be a king, worthy of his title.

The sun shone in the northern sector. Women with offer-ings, the Pandavas, Vidura, Kunthi, Dhritarashtra, Gandhari, Yuyutsu and Sanjaya approached the dying Bhishma.

He wished them well for the last time and then closed his eyes. The greatest of all Kurus was dead.

Yudhishtira enjoyed a good, peaceful reign. His subjects loved him.

Leadership secrets

Chapter 51
Uttara's Child

Uttara

Two stony figures sat on a bench. One looked anxious and was clasping and unclasping his hands. The other was smiling and seemed to be calm. The nervous one was dressed in blue silk. The other had a crown with, curiously, a peacock feather in it. He was dressed in beautiful golden silk. Ahead of them, a palace towered. As the cries of a woman in pain increased, the two entered the palace. "Will you save the child, Krishna?" asked the nervous one. "Of course I will, Arjuna," answered Krishna.

On their way, they were joined by Satyaki. When they reached the

150

Krishna giving life to Parikshit

place from where the cries had been issuing, Kunthi rushed out, saying, "Come, come, Uttara has given birth to a dead child." The three entered the room.

Ashwathama, at the end of the war, had used the Brahmasheersha astra to kill the unborn child of Uttara.

Krishna took the dead child in his hands and used all his yogic powers to bring it back to life.

The child turned pink and started crying. The women all around smiled and took turns at holding the beautiful baby boy.

Krishna, tired after using all his yogic powers to revive the baby, went outside. He now needed rest. The child of Uttara and the dead Abhimanyu was named Parikshit. He was the future heir to the Kuru throne.

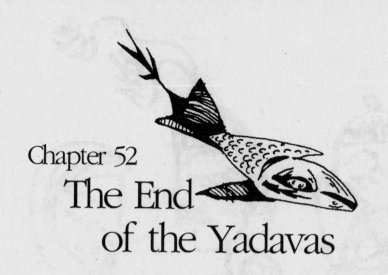

Chapter 52
The End of the Yadavas

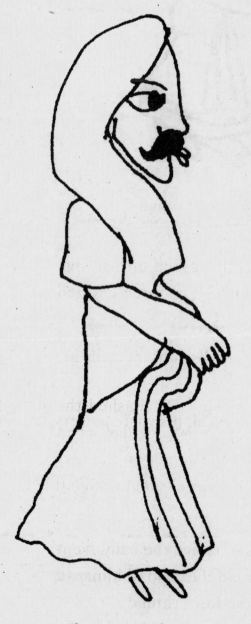

The pregnant Yadava

After the war, some sages came to stay in Mathura, the capital of the Vrishnis. After drinking alcohol, some drunken Yadavas dressed one of their own men as a pregnant woman. For a joke, they visited the sages and asked them to determine the sex of the unborn child.

The sages were much angered by this jest and pronounced an awful curse, "Indeed," they said, "this young man shall bear an iron mace which will bring about the destruction of the entire Vrishni clan."

This came true, for the young man did bear an iron mace. The bewildered youngster told this tale to Balarama who ordered the mace to be ground into a powder and thrown into the sea.

When Krishna heard this story, he banned the brewing of alcohol, since the Yadavas had done all this under the influence of alcohol.

Nevertheless, Balarama's plan was foiled. For, the waves washed the powder back to the shore and the powder grew into reeds. One day, when Krishna had gone out, the clan brewed alcohol and had a picnic on the very same beach, where the reeds had grown.

The age-old rivalry between Satyaki and Kritavarma was rekindled. A fight ensued in which the drunken men took sides. When their supply of stones ran out, they pulled at the cursed reeds. In Yadava hands, they turned into maces, spears and other weapons. Many men died. Satyaki was one of

153

them. During that time, Krishna returned and found to his dismay that Satyaki was dead. Possessed by anger, he killed all those around him. Finally only three of the Vrishni clan remained—Krishna, Daruka and Balarama, who had gone earlier into yoga.

Krishna walked into the forest. He came upon Balarama in a yoga posture. His mouth was open. A white serpent came out from Balarama's mouth. It was Sesha*. Balarama was Sesha's incarnation.

Seeing this, Krishna smiled, for he knew it was time for him to go too.

So he too sat in a yoga posture. A hunter mistook Krishna's foot for a deer and released an arrow. The arrow flew to its mark. The hunter came upon his prey and was surprised to find the dying Krishna there.

And so the clan of the Yadavas died.

When Yudhishtira heard about the fate of the Yadavas, he fervently hoped Krishna was alive, since nothing was known about his whereabouts.

He sent Arjuna to Mathura to escort the Yadava women to Hastinapura.

On the way back, Arjuna was attacked by bandits. But to his amazement, in the ensuing battle, his never-ending supply of arrows was exhausted. He then realised that Krishna was dead, for only as long as Krishna was alive, would Arjuna's divine quiver remain full.

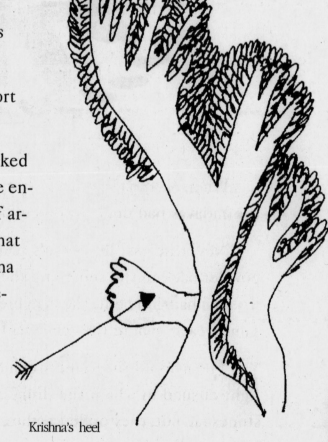

Krishna's heel

However, he managed to return safely with the Yadava women.

The Pandavas mourned for Krishna and the rest of the Vrishnis.

Chapter 53
The Elders Pass Away

"We have decided to move to the forest," Dhritarashtra announced. "Gandhari and I feel that with all our sons dead, there is nothing in this world that holds any happiness for us."

When Dhritarashtra and Gandhari announced their decision, Vidura, Sanjaya and Kunthi decided to accompany them.

To the forest

With a few servants, they made their way to a mountain slope. They pitched a hut there and decided to stay in it.

155

Yudhishtira and the others would come every few days to visit them. One day Vidura went into the depths of a forest for meditation. Sanjaya went after him and, to his horror, found that Vidura was dressed only in a loincloth. Vidura had eaten nothing at all during the past few days and was now only a bag of skin and bones.

Vidura refused to accompany Sanjaya back. Just at that moment Yudhishtira arrived and was told what had happened. He went back to the forest and found Vidura, who ran away from him. He pursued his uncle and when they stopped by a tree, Vidura transferred his spirit by yogic power to Yudhishtira's body. Now, Vidura's bodily form alone remained. Yudishtira-Vidura returned to the camp with the latter's corpse.

The forest fire

156

He told the others of what had happened. Nobody mourned for Vidura, for they knew that he was alive in Yudhishtira's body.

Dhritarashtra and Gandhari decided to move once again. Sanjaya and Kunthi seconded their decision. Kunthi had tears in her eyes when she bid the final farewell to her sons, since Dhritarashtra, Gandhari and Kunthi had told the Pandavas not to see them again. For, they said, they would manage on their own. That same evening Dhritarashtra, Gandhari, Sanjaya and Kunthi left for a higher altitude. The servants built them a hut and left some provisions. Then they returned to a hut, lower in the hills, since Yudhishtira had asked them to keep a secret watch on his elders and supply them with provisions every fortnight.

Dhritarashtra bid Gandhari to remove her blindfold, and for the first time since her marriage, she was able to see.

One day Dhritarashtra smelt something burning. Sanjaya went to investigate and found, much to his dismay, a forest fire quickly advancing. He wanted to escape with the other three. But when he heard of their decision to die in the fire, he was ready to die with them. Despite Dhritarashtra's pleas to save himself, Sanjaya stayed on. Slowly the four people—Sanjaya holding Dhritarashtra's hand and Kunthi holding Gandhari's—entered the fire.

The next day a servant came upon the four corpses and took them back to Yudhishtira who performed the last rites for the elders.

Chapter 54
The Last Journey of the Pandavas

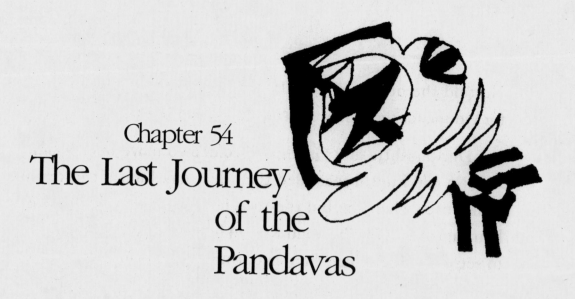

After reigning in Hastinapura for thirty six years, and having gifted Indraprastha to Krishna's grandson, Vajra, the Pandavas settled their affairs and left Hastinapura to make their last, uninterrupted journey.

They left the Kuru kingdom to Parikshit and made their way to the Himalayas. Crossing the Ganga, they came upon a treeless, barren land, with no sign of life. Day after day, month after month, Draupadi and the Pandavas continued walking in silence, in single file.

Finally, one day, something happened to break their long silence, for Draupadi fell into a deep gorge. Everybody thought that she was dead. But she lived long enough to hear the following words.

On seeing Draupadi fall, Bhima was upset. He broke the silence by asking, "Yudhishtira, why did she fall?"

Draupadi falls

Yudhishtira continued walking with his dog, who had left some home in Hastinapura to accompany the oldest Pandava on his last venture.

However, he answered in a solemn voice, clear of tears, "Draupadi had one fault, for she loved Arjuna most, instead of loving all of us equally."

Draupadi, hundreds of feet below them, heard the clear words of Yudhishtira and closed her eyes, awaiting her death.

As they ascended the mountains, the Pandavas dropped dead one after the other.

After the death of Sahadeva, Bhima repeated his earlier question. Yudhishtira answered this time that Sahadeva had to die, for he had been too proud of his wisdom.

159

When Nakula fell, Yudhishtira said, "He died because he was vain of his beauty."

When Arjuna died, Yudhishtira said that he had sworn to kill all his enemies by himself and thus insulted all the other great warriors in the land.

Finally when Bhima himself fell and shouted his question, Yudhishtira said, "Bhima, you were a great eater and you were proud of your strength. Those were your faults."

Yudhishtira continued and at the peak of Indrakila, Indra himself appeared and said, "Yudhishtira, through your righteousness and piety, you have won the pleasures of Heaven."

On hearing these words, Yudhishtira ascended the ladder to Heaven along with his loyal dog.

But on seeing the dog, Indra looked horrified and said, "You cannot take that filthy dog inside Indralokha, which is serene and beautiful."

Yudhishtira ascending the ladder

"If this loyal dog cannot go to Heaven, I will not go either" replied the

160

enraged Yudhishtira. At that moment, the dog transformed itself into Yama, the God of Death and Justice. He said, "This was just a test to find out whether you are worthy of entering Heaven. You have passed, my son." With this Indra and Yama vanished. Yudhishtira alone ascended the ladder to Heaven.

On reaching Heaven, Yudhishtira found Duryodhana and the Kauravas there. Finding no trace of the Pandavas, he asked where they were. "They are elsewhere," said Yama, who received Yudhishtira. "Come, I will show you where they are."

They reached a dark, dusty place. Not even a glimmer of light was reflected in that place. It had a musty stench and the ground seemed to be covered in filth. Yudhishtira walked warily. "Is this the place where my brothers are?" asked Yudhishtira. "Why, yes," said Yama, "they are right next to you."

Yudhishtira then asked in a low voice, "Bhima, are you here?" And Bhima answered, "Yes, I am here." Happy with the response, Yudhishtira called out, "Arjuna!" "I am here, brother," said a voice from the depths of the place. Then Yudhishtira said, "Sahadeva, are you here?" "I am here," said a serene voice. "Nakula!" said Yudhishtira, "Are you also here?" and he received an answer just like the one before.

"Draupadi," asked Yudhishtira gently, "are you too here?" and then a female voice answered, "I too am here." "Karna, the brother I never really knew, are you here?" questioned Yudhishtira. "I am here!" said a less familiar voice.

Yudhishtira turned to Yama and asked, "What place is this?"

Yama answered, "The place where people account for their sins. In other words, Hell." "Then how could that evil, vicious, tyrant Duryodhana be granted a place in Heaven?"

Yudhishtira on the golden throne

"Because he and his brothers died noble deaths. If you die a noble death, all the sins you have committed in your life are erased. Your one sin," continued Yama "was your lie to Drona and now you have accounted for it."

"Then why are my brothers, who are blameless, here?" queried Yudhishtira. "You yourself gave Bhima the answer," said Yama, referring to the time when Draupadi fell.

Suddenly a blinding flash of light appeared. The light was so powerful that Yudhishtira had to cover his eyes. The next moment, when he opened them, he saw a golden throne. Yama told him that his brothers were really not sent to hell. He had been merely testing Yudhishtira, and Yudhishtira had won. So Yudhishtira ascended the throne. On his right side, sitting on smaller thrones, were his brothers, with Karna and Draupadi. Abhimanyu, Iravat, Dhrishtadyumna, Gatotkacha and Krishna were on his left side. He looked across the hall and saw Kunthi, Vidura, Draupada, Uttara Kumar, Sveta, Virata, and Draupadi's children.

Chapter 55
After the Pandavas

Parikshit, now the king of the Kuru kingdom, ruled justly.

One day, while hunting, he came across a sage who was praying. Parikshit, who was thirsty, asked the sage for water. But the sage was deep in meditation, and did not hear the request. So Parikshit, in anger, draped a dead snake around the sage's shoulder, and left.

The son of the brahmin came out of his hut and saw the snake on his father's shoulder. Angered by the king's action, he cursed him saying, "Foolish king, you shall pay dearly for your deed. For in a few weeks time, you, Parikshit, shall be bitten by a snake."

When the brahmin arose from his penance, his son related to him the event that had taken place. On hearing this story, the brahmin reprimanded his son for having his harsh temper. He then rushed to the palace for he knew an antidote for the snake bite.

163

On the way, his path was obstructed by Takshaka, a Naga king whose family had been mercilessly killed by Arjuna. Now Takshaka wanted revenge. He prevented the brahmin from reaching the palace. Parikshit was then bitten by one of Takshaka's subjects and died a painful death. When Parikshit's son Janamejaya heard of this, he wrought destruction on the Nagas.

Later, Janamejaya was forced to abandon Hastinapura and move south to Kosambi and from then on, there is no trace of the Kurus.

However, Yudhishtira still rules in Heaven and will reign there for eternity.

Parikshit is cursed

Glossary

Akshauhini A division of the army comprising horses, chariots, elephants and 1,09,350 foot soldiers

Astra A divine weapon

Asura A demon

Chakra Vyuha An army arranged in the form of a wheel

Gandharva A divine being

Hanuman The son of Vayu, the Wind God and hence, Bhima's brother

Krauncha An army arranged in the form of a heron

Kurus The ruling dynasty of Hastinapura, referring either to the Kauravas or the Pandavas

Linga The form in which Shiva is usually worshipped

Makara Vyuha An army arranged in the form of a crocodile

Maya Magic

Sakata Vyuha An army arranged in the form of a circle

Samsaptakas Suicide squads

Sesha The name of the snake on which Vishnu reclines

Sutaputra The son of a charioteer; it is used here as a term of insult

Vasus The children Ganga threw into the river were divine beings, the Vasus, who were cursed for trying to steal a brahmin's cow. Hence, they were re-born as mortals (see The Mahabharatha 1: a child's view, Chapter 1 for details)

Vishwaroopa The divine form of Vishnu

Vrishni The name of Krishna and Balarama's clan. They were also known as the Yadavas.

Yama The God of Death and Justice, and the King of Hell.

The Pandava Alliance

Yudhishtira

Bhima

Arjuna

Nakula and Sahadeva

Krishna

Draupada

Dhrishtadyumna

Shikandin

Satyaki

Abhimanyu

Gatotkacha

Virata

Uttara Kumar

Iravat

Draupadi's children

The Kaurava Alliance

Duryodhana   Dushasana   Bhishma   Drona

Kripa   Karna   Ashwathama   Jayadratha

Kritavarma   Bhagadatta   Vikarna   Shalya

Laxmana   Sudarshana   Baahlika   Bhoori   Sala

Bhoorisravas   Susharma   Alambusha   Alayudha   Jatasura's son

The Mahabharatha 2: a child's view

© Samhita Arni 1996

First Edition 1996

Second Printing 1999

Second Edition 2002

Text & Illustration: Samhita Arni

Cover Design: Rathna Ramanathan

Production: C. Arumugam

Printer: Ind-Com Press

Tara Publishing

20/GA Shoreham

5th Avenue, Besant Nagar

Madras 600 090, India

e-mail: mail@tarabooks.com

ISBN 81-86211-71-3

Visit our website: www.tarabooks.com

OTHER BOOKS FROM TARA PUBLISHING

If you enjoyed Samhita Arni's *Mahabharatha*, you may like to look at some of our other books for children. At Tara, we believe that books are worlds in themselves. Merging strong concepts with fresh perspectives in language, art and design, Tara books offer children new worlds to delight in.

For Ages 3 and above

Babu the Waiter
Read Aloud Book

Hensparrow Turns Purple
Illustrated Folk Tale

Tiger on a Tree
Illustrated Verse

For Ages 6 and above

Excuse Me, is this India?
Verse illustrated with textile art

Anything but a Grabooberry
Illustrated nonsense verse

Leaf Life
Nature notebook

For ages 10 and above

Toys and Tales
with Everyday Materials
Activity Book

**Four Heroes and a
Green Beard**
Adventure Novel

Child Art
with Everyday Materials
Activity Book

If you want to know more about new titles from Tara, or want to be on our mailing list, visit our website **www.tarabooks.com**

Or write to us for a free catalogue at:

Tara Publishing
20/ GA Shoreham
5th Avenue Besant Nagar
Chennai 600 090
India
E-mail: mail@tarabooks.com